THE MADONNAS
OF LENINGRAD

THE MADONNAS
OF LENINGRAD

Debra Dean

WILLIAM MORROW
An Imprint of HarperCollins*Publishers*

For Cliff,
my companion on the journey

But now I know, while beauty lives
So long will live my power to grieve.

—ALEXANDER PUSHKIN

This way, please. We are standing in the Spanish Skylight Hall. The three skylight halls were designed to display the largest canvases in the collection. Look up. The huge vault and frieze are like a wedding cake, with molded and gilt arabesques. Light streams down on parquet floors the color of wheat, and the walls are painted a rich red in imitation of the original cloth covering. Each of the skylight halls is decorated with exquisite vases, standing candelabra, and tabletops made of semiprecious stones in the Russian mosaic technique.

Over here, to our left, is a table with a heavy white cloth. Three Spanish peasants are eating lunch. The fellow in the center is raising the decanter of wine and offering us a drink. Clearly, they are enjoying themselves. Their luncheon is light—a dish of sardines, a pomegranate, and a loaf of bread—but it is more than enough. A whole loaf of bread, and white bread at that, not the blockade bread that is mostly wood shavings.

The other residents of the museum are allotted only three small chunks of bread each day. Bread the size and color of pebbles. And sometimes frozen potatoes, potatoes dug from a garden at the edge of the city. Before the siege, Director Orbeli

1

ordered great quantities of linseed oil to repaint the walls of the museum. We fry bits of potato in the linseed oil. Later, when the potatoes and oil are gone, we make a jelly out of the glue used to bind frames and eat that.

The man on the right, giving us a thumbs-up, is probably the artist. Diego Rodriguez de Silva y Velázquez. This is from his early Seville period, a type of painting called *bodegones,* "scenes in taverns."

It is as though she has been transported into a two-dimensional world, a book perhaps, and she exists only on this page. When the page turns, whatever was on the previous page disappears from her view.

Marina finds herself standing in front of the kitchen sink, holding a saucepan of water. But she has no idea why. Is she rinsing the pan? Or has she just finished filling it up? It is a puzzle. Sometimes it requires all her wits to piece together the world with the fragments she is given: an open can of Folgers, a carton of eggs on the counter, the faint scent of toast. Breakfast. Has she eaten? She cannot recall. Well, does she feel hungry or full? Hungry, she decides. And here is the miracle of five white eggs nested in a foam carton. She can almost taste the satiny yellow of the yolks on her tongue. Go ahead, she tells herself, eat.

When her husband, Dmitri, comes into the kitchen carrying the dirty breakfast dishes, she is poaching more eggs.

"What are you doing?" he asks.

She notes the dishes in his hands, the smear of dried yolk in a bowl, the evidence that she has eaten already, perhaps no more than ten minutes ago.

"I'm still hungry." In fact, her hunger has vanished, but she says it nonetheless.

Dmitri sets down the dishes and takes the pan from her hands, sets it down on the counter also. His dry lips graze the back of her neck, and then he steers her out of the kitchen.

"The wedding," he reminds her. "We need to get dressed. Elena called from the hotel and she's on her way."

"Elena is here?"

"She arrived late last night, remember?"

Marina has no recollection of seeing her daughter, and she feels certain she couldn't forget this.

"Where is she?"

"She spent the night at the airport. Her flight was delayed."

"Has she come for the wedding?"

"Yes."

There is a wedding this weekend, but she can't recall the couple who is marrying. Dmitri says she has met them, and it's not that she doubts him, but . . .

"Now, who is getting married?" she asks.

"Katie, Andrei's girl. To Cooper."

Katie is her granddaughter. But who is Cooper? You'd think she'd remember that name.

"We met him at Christmas," Dmitri says. "And again at Andrei and Naureen's a few weeks ago. He's very tall." He is waiting for some sign of recognition, but there is nothing. "You wore that blue dress with the flowers, and they had salmon for supper," he prompts.

Still nothing. She sees a ghost of despair in his eyes. Sometimes that look is her only hint that something is missing. She begins with the dress. Blue. A blue flowered dress. Bidden, it appears in her mind's eye. She bought it at Penney's.

"It has a pleated collar," she announces triumphantly.

"What's that?" His brow furrows.

"The dress. And branches of lilac flowers." She can call up the exact shade of the fabric. It is the same vivid robin's-egg as the dress worn by the Lady in Blue.

Thomas Gainsborough. *Portrait of the Duchess of Beaufort.* She packed that very painting during the evacuation. She remembers helping to remove it from its gilt frame and then from the stretcher that held it taut.

Whatever is eating her brain consumes only the fresher memories, the unripe moments. Her distant past is preserved, better than preserved. Moments that occurred in Leningrad sixty-some years ago reappear, vivid, plump, and perfumed.

In the Hermitage, they are packing up the picture gallery. It is past midnight but still light enough to see without electricity. It is the end of June 1941, and this far north, the sun barely skims beneath the horizon. *Belye nochi,* they are called, the white nights. She is numb with exhaustion and her eyes itch from the sawdust and cotton wadding. Her clothes are stale, and it has been days since she has slept. There is too much to be done. Every eighteen or twenty hours, she slips away to one of the army cots in the next room and falls briefly into a dreamless state. One can't really call it sleep. It is more like disappearing for a few moments at a time. Like a switch being turned off. After an hour or so, the switch mysteriously flips again, and like an automaton she rises from her cot and returns to work.

All the doors and windows are thrown open to the remaining light, but it is still very humid. The airplanes buzz and drone, but she has stopped flinching when she hears one directly overhead. In the space of a few days and nights, the planes have become part of this strange dream, both tangible and unreal.

Sunday morning, Germany attacked without warning. No one, not even Stalin it seems, saw this coming. No one except Director Orbeli, the head of the museum. How else to explain the detailed evacuation plan that appeared almost as soon as news of the attack came over the radio? On this list, every painting, every statue, nearly every object that the museum possesses, was numbered and sorted according to size. Even more astonishing, wooden crates and boxes were brought up from the basement with corresponding numbers already stenciled on their lids. Kilometers of packing paper, mountains of cotton wool and sawdust, rollers for the paintings, all these appeared as if preordained.

She and another of the museum's tour guides, Tamara, have just finished removing the Gainsborough from its frame. It is not one of her favorites. The subject is a pampered woman with powdered hair rolled and piled ridiculously high, and topped with a silly feathered hat. Still, as Marina is about to place the canvas between oiled sheets of paper, she is struck by how naked the figure looks out of its frame. The lady's right hand holds her blue wrap up protectively over her breast. She stares out past the viewer, her dark eyes transfixed. What Marina has always taken to be a vacant-eyed gaze looks suddenly sad and calm, as though this woman from a long-ago ruling class can envision how her fortunes are about to change again.

Marina says to Tamara, "She looks a little as though she could see into the future."

"Hmm? Who's that?" Dmitri, unaccountably, is standing at the window of their bedroom, holding up a blue dress, fingering the collar.

"The Lady in Blue. The Gainsborough painting."

"We'd better finish getting dressed. Elena will be here any minute."

"Where are we going?"

"Katie's wedding."

"Yes, of course." She turns away from Dmitri and begins to fish around in her jewelry box. A wedding, so she should dress up. She will wear her mother's . . . the things that hang from ears. She can picture them quite clearly but can't find the word. Neither can she find the objects themselves. She could ask Dmitri where they've gotten to, but first she needs the word. Her mother's . . . what? They are filigreed gold with little rubies. She can picture them, but there is no word with the picture, not in English or in Russian.

She knows what is happening to her; she is not a fool. Something is eating into her memory. She caught the flu (last winter? two winters ago?) and nearly died. She who had prided herself on never being sick, who survived the starvation winter, was too weak to stand. Dmitri found her at the foot of the bed, collapsed. She lost whole days, a blank week, and when she returned to the living, she was changed.

This is her explanation. There is another. After Dmitri found her pocketbook in the oven, they went to a doctor and he asked her questions. It was like taking her exams at the art academy again, calling up answers to a barrage of random queries posed

7

by her professors. Name the major artists of the Florentine school and several of their works, including the dates and provenances. What is today's date? Describe the technical processes and materials used in the creation of fresco. I'm going to name three objects and I want you to repeat them back to me: street, banana, hammer. Identify which of the following works are now in the permanent collection of the State Museum of Leningrad and which are in Moscow at the Fine Arts. I'd like you to count backwards from one hundred by seven. Can you repeat back to me the three objects I mentioned a moment ago?

She passed her exams with distinction. But the doctor, though kind, was not impressed. He explained that she is elderly and her confusion is one of those unfortunate but not uncommon alterations that come with old age. She and Dmitri were given a packet of materials and a sheaf of prescriptions and counseled that patience and vigilance was their best course.

Because she sometimes forgets to turn off the burners, she uses the stove now only if Dimitri is present, and then only to heat water for tea. Even the dishes she knows by heart have ended up ruined so often, a cup of flour missing or something mysterious added, that she rarely cooks anymore. Dmitri has assumed most all her jobs, not only the cooking but the marketing and the washing as well. And then there is a girl who comes in and cleans, though this is almost more than Marina can bear. She tries to help the girl, or at least to make her tea, but the girl insists that she was hired to do a job and Marina should just relax. "Just put up your feet and be a queen," the girl urges. "That's what I'd do." Marina tries to explain that no one should be idle, spitting at the ceiling while others work for her, but it's no use. They have finally reached a compromise in which the girl allows her to dust.

Dmitri has laid out her clothes on the bed: a pair of slacks, a knit top, and a sweater.

She doesn't want to criticize him, but she feels sure that this is too casual. Dmitri has never had a sure sense of the right thing to wear. Left to his own devices, he might pair brown slacks and a red checked shirt with black dress shoes. She never went so far as to lay out his clothes, but she would make discreet suggestions, steering him to another tie or telling him how much she liked him in a particular shirt.

"Maybe I should wear a dress?" she asks.

"I guess you can if you wish, but I think this would be more comfortable. It's a long drive."

"And then we will change for the wedding?"

"The wedding is tomorrow. Today, we're going to the island. Tonight, there's a dinner to meet Cooper's family."

"I see." She doesn't see at all, but for the moment she will stop trying.

"Come on, darling, lift up," he says. She raises her arms, and he tugs her nightgown up over her head. When her head reemerges, she sees a naked body reflected in the mirrored closet door. It is a shock, this withered old carcass. Most of the time, she doesn't look. But when she does, this image she sees, while vaguely familiar, is not herself. It is a body she remembers, though, something about the mottled skin, pale as a fish and nearly translucent. The way the skin drapes loosely from the arms and knees. And the sagging, empty breasts. The pouching stomach. It is like the body she had during the first winter of the siege. That's it. Some differences, of course. It is softer, for one thing, without the sharp bones. But it is as alien a creature as that other body. Mulish, too, resisting her will with the same indifference, as if it really did belong to someone else.

She steps gingerly into the underpants Dmitri holds at her feet. When he holds out her bra, she lifts each breast up and settles it into a cup. At her back, she feels his arthritic fingers struggling to connect hooks with eyes.

It occurs to her that she is probably as old as Anya, one of the Hermitage babushki. There was a fleet of old ladies on the staff at the Hermitage, mostly attendants who sat in the rooms, keeping an eye on the paintings and cautioning visitors not to touch the art. Anya was ancient. The old woman could recall the day Alexander II was assassinated, and would tell Marina fantastic stories about the parties the empress held in the Winter Palace. Anya was a remnant of the old capitalist world, a time that had seemed to Marina as far in the past as ancient Greece. Now, reconsidering, she thinks it may have been only some thirty or forty years before her own birth, not long at all, really.

"When was Alexander the Second killed?"

"Oh, for . . . I don't know, Marina." She hears the flash of irritation in her husband's voice. He is still grappling with her bra. She must try to stay present.

"They don't all of them have to be closed," she tells him.

"I've almost got it." His face is hidden behind her back so she can't see his expression, but she doesn't need to. When he concentrates like this, he chews his lower lip.

"What shall we eat for lunch?" she asks brightly.

"Elena is picking us up. Then we're driving up to Anacortes. We'll eat something on the ferry, probably."

"Yes, I know," she lies. "But we might want to make sandwiches to take."

He snaps her bra strap triumphantly and rises up, appearing in the mirror behind her. He, too, has been transformed, her handsome young husband replaced by this elderly, white-haired man. It's as though his face has melted, puddles of loose skin forming under his eyes, the once firm jaw dripping into wattles. His ears are as long as a hound's.

"Okay, what's next? Top. Arms up, missus." She raises her arms again and they both disappear.

Here we are, the Hall of French Art. The room is delicate as a suspended breath, the pale dove-colored walls curving under neoclassical vaults, the inlaid floors a minuet of repeating circles and turns. And over here, against the long wall, is a young girl in a beautiful heavy satin gown. In the shadows, half-hidden behind a door, is her young man, and he is kissing her cheek. Though she hasn't seen us yet, like a deer she is alert, listening intently, expecting to be interrupted at any moment by the women in the next room. The girl is poised to flee. The long, sinuous line of her torso stretches away from the delicate contact of the kiss, through her outstretched arm, and then evaporates into the transparent folds of a scarf.

Fragonard called this *The Stolen Kiss,* but the boy is not stealing something from her. It is the moment that is stolen before she is called away.

It is like disappearing for a few moments at a time, like a switch being turned off. A short while later, the switch mysteriously flips again. When her eyes blink open, her friend Dmitri's face is before her. She has the sense that he has been watching her.

They have hardly seen each other since the start of the war. Even though his battalion has been drilling in Palace Square for the past week, though she has heard the shouted orders and the drumbeat of marching feet through the open windows of the Hermitage and known that he was at most a few hundred meters away, there simply hasn't been time.

"I came to take you out. I don't have to report to the barracks until morning, and I want to take you out for dinner."

"Dinner? What time is it?"

"Almost nine."

"In the evening?" She is always disoriented now. The Hermitage staff has been packing almost round the clock for weeks and weeks now, eating sandwiches brought into the galleries, slipping away only to use the toilet. In the first week, they crated more than half a million pieces of art and artifacts. And then on the last night of June, an endless parade of trucks carried away the crates. A train, twenty-two cars long and armed

13

with machine guns, waited at the goods depot to spirit the priceless art away, its destination a state secret. Walking back through the rooms, through wastelands of shredded paper, Marina had averted her eyes. Many of the older people wept.

But that was only the visible tip of the collection, the masterpieces on permanent display. Since then, they have been packing up hundreds of thousands of additional items, lesser paintings and drawings, pieces of sculpture, jewelry and coins, collections of silver and shards of pottery. A second train will depart in two days, and there is still no end in sight.

Nevertheless, for no reason that Marina can imagine, she has been relieved until tomorrow morning, when she must report back for her ARP duty as a fire warden. Dmitri has made some kind of arrangement with the woman from the Lomonosov Porcelain Factory who is directing the packing of breakables; he will tell her no more than this, and Comrade Markovish will say only that Dmitri has promised to name their first daughter after her. She winks at Dmitri and adds, "But he has not asked me my given name."

"I'm so sorry, Comrade Markovish. What is your name?"

"Ah, too late, Comrade Buriakov," she teases. "The deal is already made." She turns to Marina. "Go on. Just don't say anything to the other girls. I can't spare another hand."

She and Dmitri pass through room after room, weaving through a maze of sealed and labeled crates and past dozens of women lined up along tables filled with porcelain or kneeling on the floor in a forest of silver candelabra. She is ashamed to be leaving for no better reason than a meal, but when they step out into the air and she feels the breeze washing off the Neva River, her shame is forgotten. She sucks the bracing air deep into her lungs and feels herself revive. Except to run up to the roof every time the air raid sirens shriek, she has hardly set foot outside, has been home only a few times, and only then for just long enough to bathe and to change into fresh clothes that her aunt has washed out for her.

"Where are we going?" she asks.

"You shall see," he says mysteriously. He takes her arm and guides her through knots of evening strollers, across Palace Square, under the triumphal arch, and over onto Nevsky Prospekt, the main thoroughfare. In the space of a few weeks, the city has been transformed. The spire of Peter and Paul Cathedral is draped in camouflage rigging, the Admiralty tower spattered with gray paint. They pass shop windows that are crosshatched with strips of paper to prevent their shattering in the event of shelling. The window of a pharmacy is papered with a lacy design of flowers and crosses as elaborate as a Fabergé egg. After a few more blocks, Dmitri turns the corner onto Mikhailovskaya Street and stops outside the front entrance to the Hotel Grand Europa. Its plate-glass windows are hidden behind a wall of sandbags, but the front doors are open and she hears music coming from inside.

"Oh, no, Dima. I can't go in there. Look at me." The Hotel Grand Europa is legendary for its elegance, and she is still wearing her blue work smock.

"You look fine," he says. "What do you care what they think? Do you know anyone in there?"

"But it's horribly expensive."

"It is. But what am I saving my money for?" The question is not rhetorical; he is waiting for her to answer.

As though he could read her thoughts, he says, "I'm not

being foolhardy, Marina. I might as well spend it now. I suspect the ruble won't be worth an empty eggshell by the time I get back." He takes her hand. "Please humor me. This is a special night."

She can't imagine what is special about tonight, except that every night is special now. Every day, every night since the war began has become infused with a new intensity, the awareness that the world is about to change. It is strangely exhilarating. There is the possibility that when this is all over, the Soviet Union will be a better place. She is ready for change, any change.

The grand Art Deco dining room is buzzing, its tables full. Astonishing the way the world can tilt on its axis and yet people continue to walk upright, to go about their days, eating their dinners in restaurants, making their plans. Except for the incongruity of gas masks hanging from the necks of the finely dressed patrons, one might think the war looming outside were a fiction. A harpist plucks delicate music from the air, and palm trees waft in the colored light of a stained-glass skylight.

The maître d' guides them through the room to a table in a corner. He pulls out Marina's chair, and with a flourish snaps open a linen napkin and drapes it across her lap. Like magic, a waiter appears at Dmitri's elbow.

Dmitri orders champagne and osetra caviar, but the waiter takes stock of the young couple and confides that really, the caviar is not worth the thieves' rates being charged these days. He glances around discreetly. "Secretary Kuznetsov himself was here for dinner earlier, and I told him precisely the same thing. He had instead a very nice fish solyanka, followed by sturgeon in cream sauce with potatoes and a salad of cucumbers and tomatoes." Dmitri thanks the waiter and agrees that they cannot do better than to follow the Party secretary's wise choice.

It is indeed a delicious dinner, and in spite of her exhaustion, Marina finds herself enjoying it immensely. Dmitri is quiet, but Marina fills the silences by telling him about the progress of the work at the museum.

"I'm packing things I've never seen before. I just had no idea. You go on your usual routes through the museum, seeing the same things every day, and you forget how much more is not on display. I don't think anyone, except Orbeli, of course, had any idea just how much there was to evacuate. It's overwhelming sometimes.

"This morning, I had an eerie moment," she confides. She would never admit this to anyone but Dmitri. "I was packing a set of eighteenth-century Belgian Delft. Each plate has a different scene from this particular town. They are so detailed, almost like paintings, except all blue and white. For hours it was just blue and white, blue and white, plate after plate, all these detailed little scenes of houses and canals and milkmaids. And I suppose I was daydreaming because I was wrapping this one plate—it pictured the front of a house, and there was a splotch of bright red on the door. And I thought that was odd, but maybe it was a religious reference. But then the next plate, as I was looking at it, suddenly there was a splash of red in the water of the canal. And then more red. And then every plate I picked up, when I looked at it, blood appeared in the scene. The hair on the back of my neck stood up and I got a little panicky until I realized it was coming from me. My nose was bleeding. Nothing alarming, it's just from leaning over from the waist for too long. It's happening to everybody, but I suppose I was so tired, it just didn't occur to me. I know it sounds silly, something for the hens to laugh at, but I had a moment when I thought I was having a vision." She smiles at her own ridiculousness.

"I'll be so glad when we're done with the porcelain. It's so delicate, it gets on my nerves. I swear, there must be thousands of teacups alone. You should see them, Dima. Some are so thin, light shines through them. And we've run out of cotton wadding, so each one has to be wrapped in paper and packed in more shredded paper, and they look like they'll break if you breathe on them. And then there's all the plates and saucers and serving pieces. One could invite all of Leningrad to dinner and not run out of plates."

She stops when she notices that his thoughts seem to be elsewhere.

"I'm sorry," she says. "We've hardly seen each other for days, and I'm babbling about dishes. You look tired, too. Are they working you very hard?"

He studies the backs of his hands for a moment before he meets her eyes again. "We're leaving in the morning."

She is shocked into silence. They have been training for only ten days, not the month that was expected, and these are not soldiers but volunteers in the People's Army, mostly middle-aged men with no military experience. Though Dmitri is younger than most of his comrades, he doesn't look any more convincingly like a soldier. He is wearing his usual collarless shirt, and a pair of light canvas trousers that hang loosely on his lanky frame. A paperback is tucked into his pants pocket, a pencil in his shirt pocket. With his long, limp hair and wire-rimmed glasses, he looks exactly like what he is, a graduate student of literature who has only read about war.

18

"How can you go so soon? You don't even have a uniform yet," she says, as though a uniform might help the illusion.

He pats his armband with the insignia of the People's Volunteer Army. "We don't need uniforms, Marina." Then he adds, almost to himself, "What we could use are a few more rifles."

The waiter has brought their tea. She cups the warm porcelain in her palms, blowing off the steam and staring at the tea leaves on the bottom.

"Where are you going?" she finally asks.

"We're not allowed to say, but you can certainly guess."

He must mean the Luga line. Every morning now, news comes of the retreating Red Army. Some speculate that they are falling back merely as a ploy to draw the Germans deep into enemy territory and then to surround them. But whatever the reason, the Luga River is where the army will have to stand fast. About eighty kilometers to the south of the city, it is the last stronghold of fortifications between the Germans and Leningrad. In preparation, thousands of citizens have been drafted to dig trenches and construct gun battlements there. Every day, a few more packers at the Hermitage are taken from their work, handed shovels, and put on the trains heading south. Even high school children have been recruited for the work.

"So long as they are sending students there," Marina reasons, "it cannot be too bad, right?" She does not want to think about how he will manage.

"I'll come back, Marina. I promise."

"What do you mean?" she asks. "Of course you will. They say a few weeks." This is the timetable that has been announced by every official on the radio and in *Pravda,* but when she says it aloud to Dmitri, she sees in his eyes that it may well be a lie.

"Perhaps," he offers. "We can hope. But war is never as easy as they promise."

The earth tilts a little more and she feels herself sliding. In all these weeks of packing and hurried preparations, it has never occurred to her to be fearful. None of it has seemed quite real. But when people leave, they don't come back. That has been her experience. That is real.

When they emerge from the restaurant, it is nearly midnight. The city is bathed in pastel shades of dusk, like a tinted postcard. The dome of St. Isaac's Cathedral is burning gold. Above them, the sky is streaked with long purple shadows.

They stroll along the embankment of the Moyka River and then into the green shadows of Admiralty Park. The lawn has been plowed up into long rows of air raid trenches. He stops beneath a plane tree and turns to face her, looking solemn.

"I have something for you." He reaches into the breast pocket of his shirt and pulls out a tiny gold ring set with an opal.

"I don't know if it's your size. The woman who sold it to me had hands that looked like yours." He fingers the ring uncertainly.

"Would you marry me? Not now. But when I return?"

She has never given any thought to marrying Dmitri. Her romantic fantasies have always featured a future lover whose appearance and qualities were an enticingly hazy mystery, not the boy who has been her companion for nearly a decade.

She was eleven years old when they arrested her father. Three months later, the black van came back for her mother, and her life as she had known it ended. She was taken in by her mother's brother and his pregnant wife and was put in a new school where no one knew of her or her family. If anyone should ask, Uncle Viktor instructed her, she should say that her parents were away on an archaeological dig. Within a few weeks, though, the rumors had caught up with her. The circle of her new schoolmates stepped back and stranded her in a widening ripple of whispers. And there beside her was Dmitri.

His father had been arrested shortly before hers, but unlike Marina, Dmitri was quietly defiant. He taught her by example not to cringe at the sly insinuations of teachers, to hold up her chin when others treated her as though she might infect them with a disease. When she confessed to wanting to be popular, he laughed, though not meanly, and told her that only ordinary people were popular. "You might as well accept it, Marina," he had said. "Even if your parents were Party members, you would never fit in. You're unusual. That's better than popular if you have some courage."

She suspected she didn't have much courage, but neither did she have much choice. He was right. All through school, she had tried to blend in, and had managed, if not to fit in, then at least not to call attention to herself. But after her parents were charged with political dissidence, she was marked, and even her harmless traits and idiosyncrasies became fodder. She was left-handed and red-haired, both signs of a disorderly and deficient character. She sometimes hummed to herself unconsciously, or, worse, she drifted off in class, only to be called back to attention by the sounds of her classmates tittering and the teacher barking her name. Even as her peers had gotten older and less openly cruel, she had still seen it in their eyes—that subtle pulling back when she made what seemed to her a perfectly normal observation.

It was only with Dmitri that she could breathe easily and be herself. She knew that she could tell him whatever she was thinking, that she wanted to live inside a van Ruisdael painting, for instance, and he would weigh her words gravely and then ask her if she would really be happy in a static moment, no matter how idyllic.

Later, when others their age were pairing off, the two of them began, awkwardly, to kiss and hold hands. He told her he thought she was beautiful, a remarkable idea shared by no one else she knew of other than the occasional rude stranger on the street. When he first said it, she assumed he meant that she possessed an inner beauty—he frequently spoke in these romantic terms—but no, he said, he wasn't speaking of her soul. She was physically desirable. Even so, when they kissed, she imagined that they were merely practicing for others.

Yet it seems this is where they have been heading all along, and, once again, she simply has not been paying attention.

"This is too abrupt," Dmitri says, reading her surprise. "I thought, what with the war . . ." His eyes drop to the ring, and he studies it as though looking for flaws. "I love you, Marina. I suppose I should have said that, but you must know."

She should have spoken by now. "I love you, too," she murmurs. It's true, though she realizes it only after she has said the words. Marriage to Dima. She would not have guessed this, but it seems right somehow.

"Yes," she announces, nodding. "Of course."

He smiles, relieved, and reaches for her hand. When he attempts to slide the ring onto her third finger, however, it will not go. She takes her hand back and tries to work the ring over the knuckle, then takes it off and slides it onto her pinkie finger.

"I can get it sized," she assures him. "It's beautiful." She reaches her mouth up to his and kisses him.

They lean against the trunk of the plane tree and kiss, but not as they have in the past. They kiss desperately, until their mouths are raw and pulpy. He kneads her breasts through the fabric of her smock. At first it makes her pleasantly light-headed, and then her tender nipples begin to ache. There is a look at the bottom of his eyes that is new and urgent. She feels the heat radiating off his skin, the trembling of his fingers, and a persistent hardness pushing against her thigh. When she reaches down and touches him tentatively, he groans softly and presses her hand more firmly down.

This is different. In sculpture, the male member is always flaccid, a soft little worm nested between muscled thighs.

What she knows about sex is confined mostly to what she has picked up studying art. It is an uneven education, strong on anatomy but weaker in the working details. Countless paintings depict scenes of demure courtship, a few suggest languid postcoital bliss, but, excepting a few obscure oriental pieces, there is little in between.

Dmitri suddenly stops and pulls himself away from her. Both of them are panting.

"What is it?" she whispers, fearful that she has hurt him.

"We are not dogs, Marina, that copulate in a park."

She responds, reasonably, that there is no place they can go to be alone with each other. She lives with her aunt and uncle and two young cousins; he shares a communal apartment with six other students.

He nods solemnly and repeats the stock response of the Housing Committee whenever they address the perpetual shortage of apartments in Leningrad. "Privacy is a conceit of degenerate societies." He tries to smile, though he really does seem to be in pain. "So you will be degenerate with me, Marinochka?"

She nods her consent and they slide awkwardly down onto the grass. When she feels his hands fumbling at the waistband of her underpants, she wriggles out of them and leans back. What happens next, though, takes her completely by surprise: he won't fit. He pushes and pushes, and just as she is wondering if they are going about it wrong, there is a searing pain that rips from the inside out. She gasps and holds her breath against the pain until she thinks she may black out. And then it is over and they are lying, spent, on the grass. She is almost too weak to move, and there is a terrible burning where he entered her. She reaches up under her rumpled skirt and finds the swollen folds between her thighs. They are hot and sticky, and when she pulls her hand out from under her skirt, her fingers are bloody.

"Dima," she says, and holds up her hand.

He nods. "It's normal the first time. Does it hurt?"

She nods. He pulls her closer into his arms and strokes her hair. With her ear against his chest, she can hear the pulse of his blood, the steady thump of his heart, and they seem to slow as she listens. She drifts on the surf of his blood, lolling in and out of sleep.

"Go to sleep," he says. "We have time."

The sun has hardly set for weeks, suspended above the horizon like a held breath. In this endless dusk, it is easy to believe that time is elastic. It stretches out before them, the future so indistinct that it must be quite far away.

Then it shrinks and snaps back into the present moment. The clock on the Admiralty is chiming. The light is pearly gray and the air is cool. Dmitri is jostling her shoulder. She sits up and finds that the front of her smock is wet with dew. Hours have passed in the space of a heartbeat, and it is early morning. He is leaving soon. He'd rather she didn't come to the station. Even if he wanted her to, it is after five o'clock and she is expected to report to the warden's office in less than half an hour. They can say good-bye here. It is better this way. He will write. He loves her. He will come back.

A man waiting for the trolley, a lunch pail in one hand, a newspaper under his arm, witnesses the young couple emerging from the trees of the park. The girl is heartbreakingly beautiful, her clothes rumpled, her red hair loose on her shoulders, her cheeks flushed like fruit. She fingers the sleeve of her young man's shirt, says something, stops. The young man shakes his head no. Taking both her hands in his, he speaks very earnestly to the girl. Then he kisses her lightly on the mouth, turns around, and walks away. It is then that the man sees the armband of the People's Volunteers. It is a timeless story being reenacted, repeated, over and over, for centuries. Nothing changes. Only the young couple themselves do not know this.

She stares after the young soldier for a moment, and then turns, herself, and runs in the opposite direction.

Inside the Winter Palace, at the foot of the Jordan Staircase, one might believe that time has indeed stood still, that nothing has changed for centuries. The stone pillars rise regally up into a painted sky inhabited by the gods of Olympus, and the mirrored walls seem to hold the glittering reflections of generations of imperial soldiers, their sabers glinting in the dim light, and elegant women in huge satin skirts, their bosoms draped with fat pearls, their faces hidden behind sweeping fans. Marina ascends the marble steps, up, up, up, and stops on the first landing to catch her breath.

This is where the tour begins. For two years, she guided groups of schoolchildren or factory workers through the Hermitage. They would gather here at the start of a tour, and she would welcome them to the museum and begin by noting how many visitors had passed up these stairs before them. "This staircase was designed in the eighteenth century by the architect Francesco Bartolomeo Rastrelli. Notice the lavish use of gilded stucco moldings, the abundance of mirrors and marble. And above us"—she would direct their gaze to the intricately painted ceiling fifteen meters up—"the Italian painter Gaspare Diziani has depicted the Greek gods on Olympus.

"All this Baroque splendor was intended to overwhelm visiting dignitaries with the might and wealth of Russia. But this is merely the entrance. The State Museum of Leningrad comprises four hundred rooms in five contiguous buildings: the Winter Palace, where we stand now, the Small Hermitage, the Old Hermitage, the New Hermitage, and the Hermitage Theatre. The architecture is, as you can see here, magnificent. But what is even more remarkable is what these buildings contain, the most precious collection of art in the entire world.

"In pre-Marxist society, this was considered the private property of the ruling class, but after the Great Socialist Revolution, it was liberated and returned to the workers who created it." Her sweeping gesture would direct their eyes down the grand staircase and back up again to the soaring ceilings.

"Comrades, all this is yours."

This is the official welcome, lines scripted by some Party functionary, but for her it is not empty propaganda. She herself is still amazed: they are her paintings. She is like a lover who still sees her beloved in the trembling golden light of their first meeting.

Her uncle brought her here for the first time shortly after she came to live with them. It was the day his wife went to the hospital to deliver their first child. Rather than following the old ways—leaving his niece with the women while he went off with the men and got drunk—he decided instead to bring her with him to the museum, saying that they could both pass the time better in educational pursuits. She was bitterly disappointed by this change in plans, having looked forward to seeing for herself what she had heard about only in whispers. Nothing her uncle proposed could be expected to be nearly so interesting; that much she had learned already.

Even now, she can still recall her shock, how shallow and fast her breath came, as she first walked through these gilt rooms, how each new hall opened dreamlike onto still another room. The walls were crowded with the faces of stern old men and the nude figures of young women, their bodies a hot shock of flesh. Her uncle seemed not to notice what she saw—he droned on about acquisitions and restorations and who knows what else, while around them angels fluttered in turbulent skies and serene Madonnas gazed down as they passed. And the landscapes, one after another, shimmering with light, each

frame a portal into a fresh world. Her head swam, dizzy, ecstatic, saturated with color. She was twelve years old, and this
was her first taste of passion.

The gallery is nearly bare now, but she hardly notices. She is
trotting through the silent, formal rooms, her low heels clicking
on parquet floors. The ghostly court recedes into the shadows.

She is already in the future, somewhere she can only dimly
imagine, but it is very different from what she has known.

Helen has been tracing a six-block radius around her parents' house for the last half hour, looking for a place to park. Every time she passes their house, she is reminded again of the phone conversation she had with her brother. "It's getting to be too much for them to handle," he said, and she has to agree that the house is starting to resemble the student rentals in the neighborhood, the lawn scrubby with dandelions, the hedge in need of pruning.

She's passed only one open parking space, which looked to be the exact length of the Chevy Malibu she is driving. She can't remember the last time she had to parallel park, and she doesn't feel up to an extra challenge this morning, but on the fifth loop she finally relents. What the hell, it's a rental car, she reasons. She cranks the wheel and backs slowly into the space, then realizes that she's cut it too tight and pulls back out. Behind her, a kid in a jeep hits his horn in frustration. Back and forth she maneuvers, cranking the wheel one way and creeping forward, then the other way and rolling back, until she taps the bumper of the car behind her and sets its alarm shrieking and caterwauling. Thoroughly shaken, she leaves her car hanging at an angle into the street and flees.

The plan was to get here yesterday afternoon and have a little time with her parents before they all headed up to Andrei's this morning. But all it takes to shut down a major airport these days is one hophead who panics and bolts for the gates when the screener asks a few questions. She doesn't know for a fact that's what happened; this was only the rumor that later circulated around the baggage claim carousel. What she does know is that they hung over LAX for almost an hour before the pilot came on and said something vague about a security breach. And next thing you know, they're diverting the flight to San Diego and then lining up on the tarmac behind dozens of similarly diverted planes stacked up to approach the terminal. Then there were the refugee-length lines snaking up to every ticket counter, and the smiling, dead-eyed ticket agent at the front of her line who happily informed Helen that there was a seat on a flight to Portland that left in an hour and she could connect to Seattle from there. Past midnight, too late to barge in on her elderly parents, Helen finally dragged herself to the Holiday Inn Express at Sea-Tac Airport. She spent a few fruitless hours trying to shut out the din of traffic and the thunder of engines overhead before emerging into a pink, diesel-fueled dawn, renting a car, and taking her life in her hands driving up I-5 during rush hour. She's frazzled and weak-kneed, she feels about ten years older than she did yesterday morning, and she hasn't even seen her parents yet.

So she's almost too tired to notice, when she knocks at her parents' front door, that the knob rattles and the dead bolt clicks back and forth before she hears her father calling from somewhere in the back of the house that he is coming. Eventually, the door swings open. A split second passes before she reconciles the two elderly people in the foyer with her parents. She visits at least once and usually twice a year, but every time, it comes as a surprise that they are getting old. Not getting, are. Helen notes the towel tucked around her father's withered neck and the dollop of shaving cream in his left ear.

"Lenochka," Dmitri murmurs, as he squeezes her and pecks each cheek. He turns to his wife and announces, "Elena's here." Marina's face brightens and she chirps, "Well, hello there," looking for all the world as though Helen's arrival is a surprise. A pleasant surprise, but a surprise nevertheless. Marina steps forward and looks up expectantly. As Helen embraces her, she is struck afresh by the oddness of being able to see over the top of her mother's head. She seems even shorter than eight months ago, as though she is plotting to slip out of the world under the bar.

"Come in, come in," Dmitri says, ushering Helen through the living room, Marina trailing behind.

So far as she can tell, very little has changed since her last visit. In fact, very little has changed since her childhood, beyond the glacial accumulation that comes of years spent in the same place. When she grew up, the house, predictably, got smaller and, though there were fewer occupants, more crowded. Now, every surface is layered: an old brocade sofa is festooned with crocheted antimacassars and buried under a drift of decorative throw pillows; a pair of recliners is draped in afghans. The top of the enormous old Admiral television cabinet, as well as every other horizontal surface, is crowded with framed photographs of the grandkids and knickknacks and cut-glass candy dishes. But the house still looks clean. There are no empty tuna cans or piles of newspapers.

The thought of sorting through and packing up all of this overwhelms Helen, and she can see why her parents would be so resistant. But Andrei is adamant that the time has come to get them set up in a retirement village with an assisted living facility. "Of course, they don't like the idea," he said when she last spoke with him. "Who would? But they're getting up there, Helen, and frankly, we probably should have pushed this a few years ago." He's asked her to stay on for a few days after the wedding. Get that behind them and then sit down with the folks for a little powwow. See if between the two of them, they can't make their parents see reason. It's a perfectly normal request, or it would be in some other family, but she is younger than Andrei by eight years and is the eternal baby sister, rarely informed, much less consulted. It's almost silly how flattered she feels to be approached as an equal, how eager to be an ally in what has the potential to be an unpleasant battle.

In the dining alcove, Dmitri pulls out a chair in the dinette set for his wife, another for Helen. Helen remembers doing homework at this table, the aluminum edge and boomerang-patterned surface imprinted in her brain alongside Ovaltine, Little Debbie snack cakes, and the Pythagorean triangle.

"You look tired, Elena."

"I didn't get much sleep." She looks at her father. "You look a little tired yourself." In fact, he looks more than a little tired. He looks haggard.

"Well, we can all maybe have a nap in the ferry line. But first, you should have some coffee for the drive."

"No, Papa. I'm fine."

"You're sure?"

"Positive."

He checks the wall clock. "Well, then, I better get moving. Mama's ready, but I still have to finish."

Marina pipes in, "I've been ready for hours."

"Naureen said we should leave by eight-thirty so we can catch the one o'clock ferry."

"If we miss the ferry, there's another one," Helen says.

Dmitri isn't convinced. "The lines get long in the summer. I don't want to get into the soup like a chicken. You can keep your mother company while I dress?"

"You go ahead."

"I won't be long."

"No hurry."

"On the road, we can talk." Dmitri smiles at her, his watery blue eyes holding hers for a long moment. "It's good you are home."

As soon as he is gone, Marina pops up out of her chair and disappears into the kitchen. Helen hears her opening drawers and rooting around. She follows her mother into the dim kitchen and finds her methodically opening and closing each of the over-head cabinets. Post-it notes flutter like so many prayer flags.

"What are you looking for?"

"Coffee. You want a cup of coffee, yes?" Marina opens the doors beneath the sink and peers in at the collection of rags and cleaning supplies.

"I don't need any coffee, Mama."

"It's somewhere here, but Dima keeps moving things."

"Really, I'm fine. I had some at the hotel."

"It's somewhere here." Increasingly agitated, Marina opens the silverware drawer again and then each of the drawers be-low it.

"Mama, I don't want any. Truth is, if I have one more cup of coffee, something's gonna shake loose." Marina seems determined to ignore her. "Please. Come sit down." This comes out sharper than she intended, but it stops Marina in her tracks.

"Well, if you're sure." Reluctantly, Marina follows Helen back out to the table and settles her hands in her lap. She smiles at Helen.

"So, how is your family?" she asks.

Helen finds the question odd, but she can't place why. It's nothing new to tell her mother something and find out later that she's forgotten. Helen has long since stopped taking it personally. So she repeats last week's big news, that her son Jeff has been offered a promotion. It's a great opportunity, heading up customer fulfillment for the entire Southwest division, but Helen is hoping he'll pass it up.

"I'd miss them, but it's not just me I'm thinking of. It would mean transferring the family to Houston, and then he'd be spending a lot of time training people in India."

"It's nice to have the family all in one place," Marina agrees. "But I learned you have to let them chase their dreams."

"Phoenix was hardly my dream, Mama." Her mother seems never to have appreciated that Helen's moving away was not an act of rebellion. It was her ex-husband, Don, who had insisted on picking up and transplanting her and the boys, and for no better reason than he was tired of the rain. She'd had a hard time adjusting to the heat and the ugly, sunburned suburbs with no trees. Eventually she did, and even grew to love the desert, the clean emptiness of it. But none of it—not Phoenix, not the house, not the marriage—none of it had been her dream.

Her dream had been entirely different. She minored in art at the UW, and while there, she had concocted a future identity as a working artist. The fantasy was hazy but included unencumbered days following the pulse of a painting, late nights spent in the company of other artists, arguing and laughing and drinking chianti, a disorderly, passionate existence on a picturesque houseboat or in a quaint cabin in the woods. Even at the time, she'd known that such clichés wouldn't stand up to the scrutiny of her practical parents, and she knows herself well enough now to question whether she would have had the courage to so openly court their disapproval. As it happened, she never had the chance to find out. She got pregnant and stumbled forward into a life crushingly typical in its compromises: a husband who drank his ambition into quiet submission at the end of each day, two boys whom she loved fiercely enough to quell her periodic resentment of them, a job in the city planning office that was stupefyingly boring but from which she would never be fired, a few hours of drawing squirreled away here, a class there, a local art fair, a group show. Every once in a while, her lurking discontent would surface and overwhelm her, and then she would have to lock herself in the bathroom and run the tub, weeping under the thunder of the water. Lying submerged up to her nostrils like a crocodile, she would plot her escape: after the boys grew up and moved out, she would leave Don. She would throw off the yoke of her parents' caution, quit her job, and commit herself wholeheartedly to her art.

Then, surprise, Don left first, beating her out the door six months before their younger boy graduated from high school. Their son Kyle was already living in Los Angeles, and in the fall, when Jeff packed up his TV and computer and moved into a dorm at Arizona State, she was suddenly, unexpectedly alone.

She could do whatever she wished. There was no one to

answer to and no one to blame. She felt—not free exactly, that was not the word. More like abandoned.

Worse, it turned out that she was incapable of making the ripping, headlong leap out of the familiar that she had been planning for years. Instead, she has been slowly edging forward in a series of tentative half measures. She stayed in the house but converted the rec room to a painting studio. She stayed at her job for the health insurance but treated herself to a trip to Florence last year. Sometimes she stays up until four in the morning and leaves jars of paint thinner and brushes on the kitchen counter. At this rate, she figures she'll be living the dream by the time she's, say, seventy.

But she can't explain any of this to her mother. Compared with her brother, the doctor, Helen is the wild child. Picking up and moving to the middle of a desert is just the kind of thing Andrei would never do. She can't make her mother understand her, but she can't give up trying, either.

"For better or worse," Helen says, "I moved to Phoenix because I was trying to be a good wife."

Marina smiles at her benignly. "You are, dear, I'm sure."

"What?" Helen feels a little outside of her body, that light-headedness that comes of traveling and going without sleep. "I've been divorced almost ten years, Mama."

Her mother doesn't miss a beat. "Has it been so long? It's strange how time seems to fly away, yes? Poof, and it's another year."

Helen nods. "I was just thinking that."

Even before the all-clear siren has died in their ears, crowds are streaming up out of the air raid shelter and back onto Nevsky Prospekt, rushing to reclaim their places in line. One by one, they stop and raise their faces to the sky.

It looks like snow, drifts of snow falling from the German plane. As the white flakes float closer to earth, they resolve into squares of paper. They catch on currents of air, darting and sailing like tiny kites. Marina watches scores of children leap and grab at them with a mixture of terror and delight. Her little cousin Tatiana is tugging at her hand to escape, but Marina knows better than to let go of her in this crowd.

One of the leaflets seesaws through the air and lands at their feet, and Tatiana snatches it up like a prize. Marina reads over her shoulder. Printed in bold typeset, it says, "Wait for the full moon!" In smaller type, the message warns the reader that Leningrad cannot be defended, that German troops will destroy the city "in a hurricane of bombs and shells."

"What does it mean about the full moon?" Tatiana asks.

"I don't know."

"Papa, what does it mean about the full moon?" Tatiana holds up her souvenir to her father, who has appeared through the crowd. Aunt Nadezhda lags a few steps behind, with the boy, Mikhail, in hand.

Uncle Viktor's face turns angry as he reads. "They think we are backwards, that we'll be frightened by superstitious garbage." He crumples it and throws it to the sidewalk, grinding it under his boot.

Marina is surprised by the gesture. She has never heard her uncle so much as raise his voice with his children. But everyone is on edge these days, and unsuspected passions are flaring in the most unlikely of people. It has been a particularly trying day, and though Viktor continues to be the voice of reason, repeatedly reassuring Nadezhda that this is for the best, that the children will be safe, his case has not been helped by all this bedlam and hysteria.

The authorities have stepped up the evacuation of children, and every day now, thousands more are sent by bus and then train into the countryside and as far away as the Urals. Complicating matters, children who earlier were evacuated, stupidly, into the path of the enemy are now being returned to the city to be sorted out and reevacuated to the east. So, alongside the families who showed up this morning to see their children off are swarms of unaccompanied youths, a hundred to every adult, and mothers who troll the crowd, calling out names and pestering authorities, trying to locate the children they sent off to camps in the first days of the war.

Following the air raid, officials with megaphones attempt to restore order and to locate those whom they had already processed when the air raid sounded. They call out numbers and check names off their clipboards and urge the tide of people back into lines. Arguments blister into ugly scenes as people claim or dispute their places.

Viktor tried to persuade Nadezhda to stay home this morning, and even pulled his niece away from work to help him escort the children to the evacuation center, but Nadezhda wouldn't hear of being left behind. She usually defers to her husband on everything, from the amount of onion to put in the soup to the cut and color of her own clothes, but the prospect of losing her children has made her defiant. Twice in the past weeks she has managed to forestall their departure, first by pretending that Mikhail had a fever and later by simply ignoring the official orders. Even now, as they find their place in a line stretching down the avenue, she is renewing her campaign, her worst fears fueled by a conversation she had in the shelter with another mother.

"She's been here every day for a week now, but nothing. Her two girls were sent to Kingsiepp, Viktor," Nadezhda adds in a whisper. Terrible rumors are circulating that a children's camp was bombed by the Germans.

"You mustn't believe everything you hear. You don't know this woman, Nadezhda. For all you know, she might be a sympathizer." The radio has warned citizens to be vigilant against those who would aid the Fascist cause by sowing fear. Since the Luga line was broken, a firestorm of rumors has spread through the city—German spies parachuting into the city at night, the slaughter of women and children at the front—but Viktor contends that it is all hysteria.

"A pilot who was shot down last week confessed that Germans are deserting the lines," Viktor says. "The army will drive them back shortly, and when the Luga is secured again, they can bring the children home again. They'll be home in two weeks at the most."

"Then why not keep them here?"

Viktor throws her a warning look and glances around. In a muted voice, he continues. "It's merely a precaution, Nadezhda. But look at what's happened in London. We can't discount that possibility here."

"Bombs can fall anywhere." She is on the verge of tears again.

"This is not a matter of choice, and there's no point in discussing it further." To emphasize his point, he takes Mikhail from Nadezhda's arms and hands him off to Marina.

Aunt Nadezhda says something, but it is too soft for Marina to make out. It doesn't matter. She will certainly not win—Viktor Alekseevich Krasnov is a renowned scientist, a man who believes that there is always a single truth, which can be arrived at by reason, and when one arrives, he will be there waiting. Still, Nadezhda is putting up more of a fight than Marina would have imagined she was capable.

Mikhail begins to whimper, in seeming sympathy with his mother.

"What is it?" Marina asks.

The boy pauses to consider the question, poised on the cusp of crying.

"Do you have to use the toilet?"

He shakes his head. "I wanted to bring Bubi, but Papa said I can't. He says that cats don't travel well."

"Your papa is right. Bubi is better off staying at home."

"But I don't want him to get killed by a bomb."

"He's not going to get killed by a bomb. Bubi is a very smart cat. Besides, he has nine lives, so he will be fine."

Mikhail seems to accept this explanation, but his older sister is eyeing Marina suspiciously. Tatiana is beginning to take after her father, adopting his serious expressions and constantly questioning, weighing the accuracy of the fairy tales Marina tells them at night and challenging every turn in the narrative. *Why* did the witch cast a spell on the children? *Why* did she go to sleep for seven years? *Why* were they happy forever after?

Marina looks around for something to distract them, and proposes a game. She will choose a letter and they must call out all the things they can see that start with that letter.

Tatiana calls out word after word while Mikhail can only look where she points and repeat her like an echo. Marina coaches him with whispers. What is that man wearing over his shirt? *Sweater.* Good. What's that over there? *Streetlight.*

With each letter, other children in the line join in until they have gone through the entire alphabet. Then she starts repeating the letters.

It is nearing dusk when the first bus in a convoy splashed with dirty gray and green camouflage paint pulls away from the curb and rumbles down Nevsky. Nadezhda has opened the larger of two suitcases and unfurled a blanket, unpacked food meant for the trip. Mikhail has eaten and is now curled against her bosom, his face slack with sleep. An hour ago, Viktor left to find someone in charge and get an estimate of how much longer they will be here, but Nadezhda doesn't care. She is content to take up residence on the sidewalk if it means she may stay with her children.

Tatiana and Marina eat sausage and crackers and watch the buses as they rumble past. Women trot alongside, frantically waving at the occupants, children whose faces are pressed against the glass in various expressions from grief to stunned oblivion. The buses' headlights are glowing a dim blue. Black-out blue.

"Why are the headlights blue?" Tatiana asks.

"So the Germans can't see them."

"Why can't the Germans see blue?"

"Because they have blue eyes."

Tatiana considers this, decides it sounds reasonable, and nods solemnly.

Another bus rolls by, lifting a wash of leaflets in its wake.

"It looks like a parade with confetti, don't you think?" Marina observes.

"People don't cry at parades."

"No, I guess not."

"They don't," Tatiana says with authority.

Across from Helen, her mother is staring blankly out the window of the ferry. Her features are expressionless—who knows what she is thinking—but it doesn't seem to bother her to sit here in silence. Underneath a flat, bright sky, the horizon of another island undulates slowly as they pass, a velvety yellow hill unrolling in the window like a slow-paced travelogue. Helen can feel a vague roiling in her gut. It might be seasickness or it might be a growing unease, a suspicion that something is wrong.

It's not that her mother has ever been remarkably linear. Still, she just seems a little spacey. Like the business this morning with the coffee and then that remark about Helen's family. Almost as though she were making conversation with a stranger. Or on the drive up, when out of nowhere she reminded them of a trip they took to Lake Chelan when Helen was eight and Andrei was in high school. There was nothing wrong with the story; it just came out of left field.

"Mama?"

Marina turns from the ferry window and seems surprised that Helen is still here. "Hmm?"

"Are you okay?" Helen asks. "You seem a little distracted."

"I'm sorry, dear." Marina waits expectantly, ready to hear whatever it is that Helen has to say.

"No, it's all right." Helen draws in a deep breath, wondering just how to broach this. "What I meant is that, in general, you seem kind of distracted. How are you feeling?"

"I'm okay."

Helen looks at her mother and concedes to herself that her mother does look fine. Older, sure, but not especially frail or sickly. So, it could be in my head, she thinks. After all, I'm not exactly on top of my game today.

And then her mother adds, almost as an afterthought, "You know sometimes I forget some things. I told you I was sick?"

"Sick?" Helen's heart seizes.

"I had the flu. And the doctor gave me some medicines."

"The flu? Mama, are you talking about two years ago?" Her mother, who is famously never sick, had a bout of the flu the winter before last. The doctor prescribed something, but she got sicker; she grew delirious and drifted in and out of consciousness for two days. As it turned out, her mother was allergic to codeine and, at eighty, had never before had cause to find out. But what this has to do with anything is anyone's guess.

"Yes, two years ago," Marina concurs. "They seem to help my memory."

Helen is thoroughly confused. "What helps?"

"The medicines."

"The codeine?"

Marina's expression betrays her frustration. "No, the other medicines," she says, enunciating each word. She looks around. "Where's Dima?"

"Beats me." Her father left more than half an hour ago to

use the men's room, something that really shouldn't have taken this long. "Maybe he's getting a cup of coffee."

"But he will come back?" A shadow passes over Marina's face, as though she is afraid that after nearly sixty-five years of marriage he might suddenly abandon her, say he's going to the men's room and never return.

"Of course he will." I'm not imagining this, Helen thinks. This isn't me. "I'll go look for him," she offers. She has a few questions for her father anyway. "Do you want anything?"

"No, thank you. I'm okay." She folds her hands in her lap to demonstrate her contentment.

Helen finds Dmitri standing at the rail of the stern, facing the water. A wake spreads out behind the boat like a long green tail.

"Pretty, isn't it?" Helen says. "We were beginning to think you'd fallen in."

"Where's your mother?" Dmitri cranes his neck and scans the deck.

"At our seats."

He straightens as though to leave.

"Papa, what medications is Mama taking?" She keeps her voice neutral, though it's an odd question to pose casually, and, sure enough, her father stops and looks at her appraisingly.

"Why?"

"I don't know. She just seems a little—I don't know—kind of fuzzy. Don't you think so?"

"Yes," he admits. He studies the backs of his hands. "It's not her medicines. This getting old is a trial. I can't recommend it." He is smiling, but there is a weariness behind his smile that belies the joke.

"Things might be easier if you moved into a smaller place."

His mouth hardens. "I'm not ready yet to be packed off to a nursing home."

"Not a nursing home, Papa, a retirement community."

"Did Andrei put you up to this?"

As a child, she could never fib to him; his gaze was so still and patient, as though he already knew the truth and was merely waiting for her to work herself up to confessing it. Helen realizes too late that she should have let this sit until Monday.

"I'm sure he doesn't want you to do anything you're not ready for. But at least hear him out, okay, Papa? He's gone to a lot of work researching all this. Who knows, you just might see something you like."

"I know what I'll see, Elena. I have friends in these places. Walt Crawford, you remember him?" She does. Mr. Crawford was headmaster at the private school where her father taught German and Russian for almost thirty years. "Bea, his wife, she died two years ago. Bladder cancer. He's living at the Shoreside Manor. Every couple of weeks, I go up there. It's one of the good ones, four thousand dollars a month. But there's no disguise for a death camp. I'd rather to die at home."

He straightens up, signaling the end of the conversation. "Let's go. I don't want your mother to worry I've gone overboard."

If she had it in her to pursue the argument, she could point out that we'd all rather die at home, but all she can think is that Andrei will be annoyed with her for jumping the gun. Though how he hopes to move them against their will is beyond her. They are stubborn people in their own quiet way. It's the Russian blood, she thinks. She's got it herself. Her ex used to call her "the mule," and though she rebelled at the insult, she knew there was truth to it. She tends to stick with things long past the time any reasonable person would give up and move on. Case in point, her marriage. Or her art, for that matter. Anyone else in her situation would have given up the pretense and either accepted that her art was a hobby or started painting things there was a market for—landscapes and flowers or watery abstracts. Instead, she insists on doing her figures and then gets indignant that people who buy their art in the local gift shops and frame stores aren't looking to hang pictures of nude strangers in their homes. She's fifty-three: how much longer is she going to wait for a New York dealer to discover her? In their own ways, she and her parents seem to have simultaneously reached the limits of hunkering down as a life strategy.

Her mother is still staring out the window when they return.

Her father leans over and kisses the top of her head. "A penny for your thoughts," he says.

"I was thinking about Tatiana and Mikhail."

Dmitri frowns.

"Who are they?" Helen asks her mother.

"My cousins. They were only six and eight, so they were sent away."

"Sent away?"

"Evacuated. At the beginning of the war."

"Where did they go?"

Marina looks up at the ceiling for a moment. "I don't remember. The Urals, perhaps. It was snowing."

Helen waits, but apparently that is the end of the story. That's about par for the course. Her parents never talk about the war, not in English, anyway, and Helen has only the most general idea of what happened then. Her father was a soldier, and her mother was a war bride who got trapped in Leningrad when the Nazis surrounded the city. Somehow they both ended up in Germany and found each other there. That's it. As a child, she had little curiosity about her parents' youth, and they obliged by behaving as though they had never had one. When she did ask, every question got a one-sentence answer. But they won't be around forever, and it seems odd to know so little of their history.

"Were these the archaeologist's children?" Her mother was an orphan and lived with an aunt and an uncle who was a famous archaeologist, but again the details are fuzzy.

"Yes, Uncle Viktor," Marina says, nodding. "After that, we lived in the cellar."

"Who?"

"Oh, everybody. There were hundreds of people."

No explanation follows. When Helen turns to her father, he says, "Some things are better forgotten."

This is considered a minor painting, but some may find it of historical interest. Here the painter Caraffe finds his inspiration in the legend of Metellus, a Roman general who showed mercy on the innocents. We see the city has been surrounded, and at the gates, the army is preparing to storm the walls. Armored soldiers raise their bows, and half-naked corpses are strewn in front of the gates. Against the wall, a clutch of figures face the oncoming soldiers as human shields, the wife and children of a defector.

What could be more dramatic? There is no terror in this scene, though. It is a staged melodrama with the actors arranged in a carefully balanced tableau. Notice, even the vanquished are beautiful: they die in graceful poses, their injuries unseen. The neoclassical scene is strangely calm and still, the colors clean and glossy. It is war without blood and vomit, without misery—it is a picture to lure French boys to war with fantasies of ennobling self-sacrifice. Hundreds of thousands of them died for Napoleon, their frost-rotted corpses littering the snowy Russian steppes. There was no beauty, no mercy.

What she remembers is the acrid smell of burning sugar. The way it singed the lining of her nose.

When Marina emerges from the stairwell onto the roof, she can already hear the low rumble of the approaching Junkers. Schlisselburg fell on Monday, and so Leningrad is completely surrounded now, cut off from the outside world. Two nights ago, the Germans began dropping incendiary bombs, setting fires around the city. Wardens, armed with shovels and buckets of sand, have been posted in the various halls and around the perimeter of the roofs of the museum. Marina is a fire spotter, one of a pair posted to each observation platform on the roofs of the Hermitage.

She climbs the dozen steps up onto a small wooden platform. Olga Markhaeva, a curator of Netherlandish painting, is already up here. Her husband, Pavel Ivanovich, is in the same Volunteer division as Dmitri. Olga greets Marina and then hands her a pair of binoculars, which Marina hangs around her neck.

"Look," Olga commands, pointing to the south.

Through the binoculars, Marina follows the droning sound and finds a slowly approaching shadow against the clouds. All summer, there have been planes, tiny specks like mosquitoes circling and diving over the city. But this is different. She cannot make out individual planes, only a menacing phalanx of darkness.

It is not quite dark, and, standing up here on this platform, Marina feels exposed to the sky like a mouse. There is no place on the vast expanse of the roof to hide. Cold with dread, she eyes the door leading back down to the hall below. Were it not for Olga Markhaeva's presence, she doubts she would be able to resist retreating back down into the safety of the museum.

The Hermitage can't possibly be a military target, but that is no comfort. There is no sense to any of this, nothing a sane person can understand. Though in the abstract, everyone knew that the Germans were close, when the first shells came screaming into the city a few days ago, it was like a fantasy, surreal and outrageous. Stunned, people looked to each other, disbelieving. This could not be. Not here, not in Leningrad. It is lunacy. They fire long-range missiles into the city, killing women and children and old people at random. For what? And why try to burn down a city? What good is victory if there is nothing left to claim?

Marina thinks of Dmitri and his love of rational argument. What would he do with this? Perhaps there is a logic to this that can be seen only from a cool distance: the two and a half million inhabitants of Leningrad a pin on a map from somewhere in Berlin. But here she is too close to see any pattern. Looking at the horrific swarm bearing down on them, it is easier to believe the explanation on the radio: that the enemy is uniquely evil.

"There must be fifty of them tonight," Olga says. Her voice is calm, with no hint of the terror Marina feels.

The drone of the Junkers is louder. They are clearly visible now, a dozen, two dozen, maybe more. They move methodically in formation. The ack-ack guns sputter wildly, and she hears the thudding of explosives to the south. Through the binoculars, she picks out a burst of flame near the edge of the city, out by the Vitebsk railroad depot, then several more clustered together. Then the fires are sprouting in a straight line across the dark landscape of the city, springing up like rows of orange tulips. The thunder of engines envelops her, and suddenly bombs are bursting in the Neva, fountains of spray blooming up the length of the river. The platform shudders in the wake of each explosion. A searchlight sweeping the sky catches one plane after another in its path, and Marina sees the swastika on a wing directly above her.

It is not fear, exactly—that is not why she stands so rooted and still, her breath locked in her chest. She is mesmerized by the awful beauty she is witnessing. As soon as the planes are past, though, Marina realizes that her legs are trembling, so much so that she has to grip the rail of the platform with both hands in order to remain upright.

The two-way radio inside Olga's jacket is crackling. She reaches inside her jacket and pulls it out.

"Has anything hit us?" It is Sergei Pavlovich, down in the warden's office.

Olga shouts into the radio. "Just a moment. Over. Marina Anatolyevna?"

Marina looks at her and then realizes the binoculars are strung around her own neck. She releases one hand from the railing, and brings the glasses up to her eyes, but her hand is shaking too hard to steady the image. It jumps and wavers.

Olga watches her calmly and waits.

Marina releases her other hand and stiffens her grip on the glasses. She scans the roofs of the Hermitage buildings and across to the gabled roofs of the Winter Palace, where another platform is rigged. And then she checks again, slowly, methodically. Amazingly, the Germans seem to have missed the museum entirely. She directs her binoculars toward two still figures, their counterparts on the far platform. Other figures stand at their posts. No one is moving. She can't see any fires.

"Nothing. I don't see anything," she tells Olga, who relays the information to Sergei.

"Check the perimeter," Olga reminds her.

Marina sweeps her glasses up and down the embankment. Just across the river, in the gardens next to the Peter and Paul Fortress, the roller coaster has caught fire. The huge wooden structure is ablaze, a writhing dragon of orange flame. She turns and scans the buildings along Millionnaya Street and ringing Palace Square, inscribing a slow circle. Then she looks for spots of fire farther out in the range they are assigned to report on.

"There's a fire near the Trotsky Bridge, past the Trotsky, I think." Without lights, it is hard to find landmarks, but she calls out approximate locations to Olga, who relays them to Sergei.

"And another one—this one looks bad—near the Engineer's Castle."

There are nearly a dozen fires within a kilometer's radius of the museum. She relays them one by one to Olga, trying to be accurate.

"On the far side of the Moyka, near the Stroganov Palace, I think. No, wait . . ." As she is watching, she spots a fire truck already rattling down Nevsky toward the fire. But it races right past the fire and turns south onto Vladimirsky. Other trucks are moving down the avenues, their bells ringing, passing fires that burn unchecked. They are all heading south. When Marina turns her binoculars in that direction, she finds an enormous column of smoke. The plume rises high into the sky above the city. At its base, it is tinged with red.

"My god."

"What is it?" Olga is standing at her shoulder.

"I don't know. It's near the Vitebsk station." She unstraps the binoculars and hands them to Olga.

Later, she will find out that what they are witnessing is the burning of the Badayev warehouses, where the food supplies for the entire city are stored. Or maybe they know this already; maybe Sergei has reported back to them the rumors already circling the city. Tomorrow, the worst of those rumors will be confirmed. Three thousand tons of flour, thousands of kilograms of meat, a molten river of sugar flowing into the basements of the charred warehouses. She cannot know this now, but lodged in Marina's mind, as real as anything else, is the chilling certainty that they are witnessing catastrophe.

Down in the streets, there is a rushing of dark figures, the sounds of yelling, the rattle of antiaircraft fire though there are no more planes. But from up here, it seems silent, the terrible silence that might accompany the end of the world. After they have reported the fires within their range of visibility, they stand for a long stretch of time. They watch as sections of the roller coaster buckle and crash to the ground. Searchlights sweep the sky, swords of white light crossing, swishing apart, and crossing again. A full moon rises like a blood orange on the horizon. They may not leave their post, and no one comes to relieve them.

Marina wants to sit down, but Olga remains standing, erect as a soldier. Up and down the long series of roofs, wardens stand watching the distant conflagration and the smaller fires dotting the city. Their silhouettes blend into the rows of green copper statues that line the perimeter of the Winter Palace roof, warriors and gods that have vigilantly guarded the palace for nearly two centuries.

The smoke slowly drifts north, smothering the city in a dull haze. It smells strange, sickly sweet. She can no longer see flames because of the smoke, but a thick red glow seems to envelop a whole section of the city. Her eyes burn and her mouth tastes sooty.

Later, a second wave of Junkers appears on the horizon. Rather than strafing the city, they circle around the pillar of smoke like dark moths, dropping fresh rounds of fire. A few planes stray north, but they don't drop bombs.

Marina lifts the heavy binoculars to her eyes again, but before she can adjust the focus, there is a whistle, then the deafening crash of a high explosive in her ear. A shock wave blasts through her body, knocking her off her feet.

Someone is screaming. When she opens her eyes, she realizes that the screams are hers, but she is unhurt, she is fine. Her limbs surge with electricity. She stands up and looks around. Olga, too, is all right. In fact, she seems not to have moved. But something has changed. It takes Marina a long moment to place what is different. Part of the roofline of the building next door has disappeared. It is simply gone.

Rooms have been reserved for members of the wedding party at the Arbutus Hotel, a Victorian-styled inn with a dozen rooms in the middle of town. It trades heavily on its status as the oldest lodgings on the island, a distinction, Helen observes, that seems to preclude updating the furnishings. The dark-paneled lobby is furnished with a mismatched collection of cracked leather couches and high-backed armchairs and decorated with faded photographs of the island when it still had a salmon cannery and a fleet of fishing boats. Framed and yellowed signs behind the manager's desk list weekly rates in the single digits and caution guests against smoking or cleaning fish in their rooms.

Upstairs, their adjoining rooms are small and spartan, but each overlooks the harbor and has a private bath. Helen takes the smaller of the two rooms. They have a couple hours before the rehearsal dinner, enough time for short naps. She sits down on the edge of the bed. The mattress is mushy, but it doesn't matter. She's pretty certain that given half a chance she could sleep standing up. She pulls closed the curtains, sets the alarm, kicks off her sandals, and sinks back onto the coverlet.

And then her brain starts clicking through a series of

disjointed thoughts, the way it sometimes does when she's tired but has had too much caffeine. Her mother lived with her uncle in a cellar. Why would a famous archaeologist live in a cellar? Was this a normal deprivation in Soviet Russia? Maybe they were hiding, like Anne Frank, but that doesn't make sense either because they weren't Jewish. Well, she doesn't know that either, does she? People hid those things. For all she knows, she herself could be Jewish. Wouldn't that be an odd thing to discover at this point in her life.

This is ridiculous, she tells herself. It's four twenty-eight. You've only got an hour. Go to sleep.

Let's say she did find out she was Jewish. What would change, really? It's not as though she'd start keeping kosher. She's never been religious, though she flirted briefly with Catholicism. You can't throw a rock in the Southwest without hitting a Catholic church, and they're always open. During the divorce, she spent a lot of time sitting in the back pews of dark chapels. She even attended a few newcomers' classes, but she quickly discovered that it was only the imagery she liked. The doctrine was less appealing. But she did get a good series, haunting portraits of various women—a high school girl in jeans and a halter top, a middle-aged Mexican woman wearing her nurse's whites and Adidas and bifocals, a heavyset woman with an ill-fitting business suit and a ginger-colored perm— each posed as a stiff-limbed Madonna with sad, downcast eyes and an unreadable expression. She set them against a shadowy dark ground, lit only by a bank of flickering blue votive candles at their feet. Helen gave the best of these to her mother because her mother remarked on the good repetition of blues, the very thing that had pleased Helen about it. Go figure. Her mother is odd that way. She knows a great deal about art for someone who has no particular love for it. Helen was a freshman and taking her first art history class when it came out that her mother had also studied art in school, and had even worked briefly at the Hermitage museum when she was young. There was nothing in Helen's background to prepare her for this revelation; her parents had never taken her to museums or art galleries. They didn't even have any art on their walls, unless you wanted to count a couple of aphorisms done in cross-stitch, a calendar from the savings and loan with photographic scenes of Washington State, and her own drawings taped to the fridge. But one night at dinner, Helen and her mother had embarked on one of their food battles, her mother expressing what bordered on moral outrage that Helen would eat only cottage cheese when she had prepared a good dinner. Helen, in the time-honored manner of freshmen, made a little offhand remark calculated to pass over the head of her ignorant mother. Thanks to you, she said, I'm already revoltingly Rubenesque. Not only did her mother know who Rubens was, but she rallied him to her side of the argument, pointing out that many of the great painters had chosen models of Helen's proportions, not only Rubens but Titian as well. She then went on to tick off one example after another of voluptuous nudes.

Helen follows the meandering string of her thoughts for almost an hour before she finally relents, gets up, opens the curtains, and pries up the sticky sash. Leaning her elbows on the window ledge, she inhales the salt-bleached air and watches the late-afternoon ferry lumber into the dock, churning up green water as it snugs between the creosote pilings. It disgorges a fresh load of tourists, first the cyclists followed by a small army of rainbow-attired people carrying backpacks and being towed by dogs straining at the leash. Behind them, vehicles bump up the ramp one at a time, SUVs and convertibles and cars with kayaks strapped on their roofs, a couple of campers, a produce truck, a fuel truck, and finally a flatbed loaded with lumber. The street fronting the harbor swells with a cacophony of music and shouted greetings, but then the tourists slowly disappear into restaurants and trinket shops and the street settles back into a muted afternoon torpor.

She opens her suitcase, unzips the hanging bag, and starts unpacking. She has brought too much for five days, but it's hard to know what to pack for Seattle and Drake Island in August. In Phoenix, the weather is hot or hotter, but here it could be wool sweaters in the morning and sundresses by noon.

More to the point, though, occasions like this bring out all her worst insecurities. You'd think that by fifty-three she would have grown comfortable in her own skin, but she can still get as obsessive and fretful as a teenager. In anticipation of coming up here, she kept viewing herself through the imaginary lens of her stylish sister-in-law, and what she saw was a plump, faded hippie, the type who might be selling whole grain bread at the Saturday market. She bought and returned three different dresses before she found a coral linen shift and matching Nehru-collared jacket, smart and pulled together but still casual enough for an outdoor wedding. Holding it up now, she wonders what possessed her to choose this color. It's as bright as a traffic sign.

She unzips the dress, pulls it over her head, and tugs on the little jacket. There's no mirror in the room, so she goes into the bathroom and carefully hoists herself up onto the edge of the tub. Surveying her reflection in the mirror over the sink, she notes that the fabric is pulling across the bust, and the linen doesn't begin to disguise the mound of her stomach and the swells of her hips. She's spent a lifetime watching her weight, but for the past several years she's ceded one dress size after another, no matter what she does. Even after cutting back her points to near-starvation level, she is still eight pounds shy of the goal she set for the wedding. She's not even going to attempt to twist around and look at the rear view.

Someone is knocking.

She climbs off the tub and opens the connecting door to her parents' room.

"Oh. Hello," her mother says. "I opened the door, and there was another one."

Her parents' room is dark, but Helen can make out the shape of her father under the covers of the bed.

"Did you want to come in?" Helen whispers.

"Okay. Do I interrupt something?"

"No, I was just unpacking. What do you think?" She holds out her arms and does a slow turn.

"It's a beautiful color," Marina says.

"Is it too tight? I don't look like an overripe melon?"

"No. You look lovely."

"Thanks, Mama," she nods. This is her mother's stock reply. "Oh, well. No one will be looking at the bride's aunt."

Since the bombing began, some two thousand of the staff and their families—the scholars and researchers, the curators, the women who sweep the galleries and polish the floors—all have moved into the cavernous vaults beneath the Hermitage. Viktor Alekseevich Krasnov is a scholar and archaeologist renowned for his work on the digs at Karmir-Blur, and so, though all here are comrades, equals, in theory, the few square meters allotted to him, his wife, and his niece are in a corner of Bomb Shelter #3, tucked behind a pillar of the vault. With a large carpet strung from pillar to wall, the space is almost like a private room. Later, when winter comes and the walls of the vault ice over, this corner will prove to be not only damp but a degree or two colder than the middle of the vault, where the crowded workers generate a bovine heat. But already Marina has cause to regret her privilege.

She owes him everything; she knows this. When her father and then her mother were arrested and taken away, Uncle Viktor took her in and gave her his surname. He arranged for her education to continue at the university and then the art academy, and when she graduated he facilitated her subsequent appointment as a docent in the museum. He has been the model of a devoted uncle, taking a close interest in her friends, overseeing her studies

61

and the books she is reading, everything. Still, she cannot mistake this interest for affection. It is the tense act of balancing what he terms a sacred duty to his dead sister with the insidious threat Marina represents as the daughter of convicted counterrevolutionary activists. Never mind that the charges were invented. Never mind that he himself was arrested and imprisoned in 1930 on similar charges and released a year later only when Director Orbeli personally intervened on his behalf. He returned from prison with ruined lungs and a fastidious compulsion that every aspect of his life appear correct and blameless.

Half of every year, he spends in Armenia at the excavation site in the Caucasus. He leaves with the first thaw, and Marina has always associated his departure with the advent of spring. In his absence, the household becomes warmer and lighter. Nadezhda wears her hair down and dresses the children in play clothes. By summer, they are living like bohemians: eating whenever they feel hungry, staying up till all hours, and entertaining Dmitri and his friends. To be sure, when Viktor returns in the autumn, there is always a period of readjustment in the household. But even so, the relative spaciousness and privacy of their apartment makes his stiffness, his calculated inquiries and ponderous lectures, easier to stomach. Here, quarantined together in this cramped space, she can hardly endure him.

Furthermore, Viktor Alekseevich Krasnov snores.

Even with a scarf wrapped tightly around her head and a blanket pulled up around her ears, she can't muffle the sound. Following her shift on the roof last night, she was kept awake another several hours, her fatigued brain snared in the drama of his next breath. First, the long volcanic rumble. Then an uneven stretch of silence. It is like hearing the whistle of a bomb and waiting for the explosion. She can count to twenty and sometimes even thirty before he will finally gasp up more air.

He was given a complete discharge from military service on account of his lungs. Logically, this is probably what causes him to snore so loudly, though Marina can't help but think of it as an extension of his pedantic character, that even in his sleep he must be listened to. By morning, she is convinced that she could stuff a rag down his throat and not feel any guilt.

Aunt Nadezhda has brought the three of them their ration of bread and coffee. The coffee is nearly colorless, brewed from used grounds. The handful of tea leaves that Marina bought with her mother's ruby earrings was gone two weeks ago. Beautiful rubies suspended in filigreed gold. One hundred grams of tea.

"Sergei Pavlovich says that they confirmed it this morning. Uritsk has fallen." This rumor has been circulating widely, but it was too horrific to be believed. Uritsk is a mere ten or twelve kilometers from the Hermitage, a ride on the tram.

On the radio, bad news lags several days behind the rumors, but people gather around the radio in the mornings nonetheless and repeat the official pronouncements from person to person around the Hermitage shelters. Even couched in the uplifting propaganda of the Information Bureau, it is repeatedly bad news these days. It seems now that Viktor's confidence in the Red Army's easy superiority over the Germans was misplaced. It is the third week of September, and the Germans have been steadily pushing back the army, edging closer and closer to the gates of the city itself. Still, he was all too right about the bombardment. He seems to take some grim satisfaction in the robotic regularity with which the German planes reappear every night at precisely seven o'clock. If nothing else, he says, it reconfirms the rightness of his decision to override Nadezhda's terror and allow the children to be evacuated.

They have not been able to procure any news of Tatiana and Mikhail since they were evacuated, but they both hold fast to the conviction that they are still alive, that they were not among those bombed by the Germans as they fled the city. Grim rumors have come back of trains arriving in the Urals, their charred hulls filled with the burned bodies of children.

Though Nadezhda flinches at the mention of her children, she will not contradict her husband's arrogant surety that they are safe. That would be tempting fate. Neither can she bring herself to agree, so she pretends she has not heard. She hands Marina her coffee and bread and asks how she slept.

It is only because Marina is so tired that she begins to weep into the pale liquid. The older woman carefully sets down her niece's cup so none of the coffee should spill and draws the young woman into her arms like a child. She strokes Marina's hair and makes comforting shushing noises. Every sigh, every gesture, is weighted by the absence of her children.

"I'm sorry," Marina says, embarrassed.

"Nonsense. You are worried about Dima," Nadezhda says. "But you shouldn't worry. There is no time for letters. And you know how bad the army is about delivering mail. You will probably get a whole packet at once." There were letters in the first month, even if only a few scrawled lines, but Marina has not heard from him since the middle of August. His division was among those encircled after the Luga line fell, and in the chaos, many disappeared, Dmitri among them. Olga Markhaeva's husband, Pavel Ivanovich, was in the Third Division as well, but he has not been able to provide any information except to write that no one he has talked with in the unit saw Dmitri fall. Marina's shameful hope is that he is among the deserters.

"He will come home," Nadezhda says. "They will all come home soon." Then she, too, begins to weep.

Viktor stares stonily into his own cup and pretends not to notice. It is the same way that Marina pretends not to hear her aunt and uncle's furtive lovemaking, the same way that everyone pretends not to notice family quarrels or the sounds and smells of slop pails. After a moment or two, he can stand it no more. Without a word, he stands up and turns his chair around so that it faces away from the women and toward the makeshift desk at the foot of his pallet. This signals that he is now at work and not to be disturbed. Nadezhda sniffs up her tears and bites her lip.

So far as is possible in this crowded shelter, the residents cling to the routines they had before the war. It is a communal act of faith that if they adhere to the routines of their old lives, their old lives will return to them. The scholars continue to draft their papers, the students study for exams. Viktor Alekseevich Krasnov has been organizing several years' worth of his field notes in order to begin work on a history of the pre-class culture of Urartu. He diligently puts in an hour every morning before he and Nadezhda go out to work on the fortifications, then spends several more hours in the evening working by the light of an altar candle.

Marina can't get around the bulky gilded chair that Viktor has co-opted from a set Marina carried down last week from the Snyders Room.

"Pardon me," she says.

"One moment, Marina." Viktor's eyes do not leave the page he is scrawling on. Finally he reaches the end of a thought, takes a sip from the dregs of his coffee, and then stands to allow Marina to pass. He wishes her a good day. She masks her murderous feelings in a nod but cannot bring herself to return his greeting.

It is harder for Marina to preserve her old life. She was a museum guide, and now there is no one to guide and nothing to see. Every day, she walks through the abandoned picture gallery with its broken and boarded windows. Hills of sand are piled near the entrance to each room in case of fire. And on the walls are rows of empty frames, left hanging as a pledge that the paintings will return someday. Each time she enters a room, she runs through her script, mentally placing as many of the paintings as she can recall back in their frames. She moves like a ghost past the blank rectangles and describes by rote the pictures that hung inside them. She narrates the history of the paintings and the stories they tell, pointing out the range of expressions in van der Goes's mourners, the way that Velázquez used light and shadow to transform paint into a table linen with such weight and texture that one can almost feel it in the tips of one's fingers. Out of the corner of her eye, she can almost see the loaf of bread, the pomegranates and sardines, all arranged on a heavy white cloth, and the three peasants posing around their luncheon table. As always, they are boisterous. One seems to wink at her.

Today, her route to the smallest of the three skylight halls takes her through the Italian Renaissance. Here is Giorgione's *Judith*. She is so serene, so poised, that it is a shock to follow her lowered gaze down the length of her shapely leg and find beneath her foot the severed head of Holofernes.

And here is *The Assumption of Mary Magdalene into Heaven*.

66

She is flying, her startled eyes lifted up, her arms spread wide, her cloak and red sash trailing behind her. Supporting the Magdalene are a pair of full-grown angels and a flock of tiny putti, fat little cherubs hefting her on their backs and shoulders as though she were a heavy sack of grain. Domenichino has also painted strange disembodied cherubs in the sky, infant heads propped on flapping wings.

"Good morning."

The Magdalene and putti vanish, replaced by an empty gilt frame.

Anya, one of the babushski, hobbles toward Marina. If Anya wonders, she doesn't ask what Marina is doing, why she is loitering in this deserted room, staring at nothing. She stops at Marina's side, follows her glance, and nods appreciatively. "I've always liked that one, too." Then she says, "Did you hear? They've had to shut down the Kirov Works again. The German bastards got a direct hit with a delayed explosive and it's in the basement. They've got one of the girls working on it." A group of young women has been trained to defuse the delayed explosives the Germans are dropping now, and their heroics have become the subject of nightly radio broadcasts. To minimize the loss of life, they work alone, a single young woman crawling down into the bomb crater and toiling against a ticking fuse. They are the new symbols of Soviet womanhood, Judiths going into single combat with mechanized monsters, slaying the enemy to save their people.

Marina's work is less dramatic. Whatever remains in the museum that can be moved is being hauled downstairs and out of harm's way. Since the bombing started, they have carried hundreds of chairs, massive stone vases and tabletops, standing candelabra, mirrors, and couches. They are stripping the rooms bare, one by one. It is hard physical labor and nearly as tedious as the packing. Yesterday it took a dozen of them the whole day to wrestle the two onyx candelabra out of the Large Italian Skylight Room and into the basement.

Today, the other members of their crew have moved on to the Small Italian Skylight Room. All that remains are the chairs and tables that can be managed by the two women. Marina takes one end of a small divan, Anya the other. They heft it up and begin slowly retracing their steps through the gallery.

Lionello Spada, *The Martyrdom of Saint Peter*. Annibale Carracci, *The Holy Women at the Sepulchre*.

"What's that, dear?" Anya asks. "My hearing isn't so good anymore."

Marina is embarrassed to realize she has been muttering out loud. "Oh, I beg your pardon. It's nothing, a sort of game I play. To see how many paintings I can recall."

"You are building a memory palace?"

Marina has never heard of such a thing.

"They don't teach this in school anymore?" Anya asks and clucks in dismay. "When I was a girl, we made memory palaces to help us memorize for our examinations. You chose an actual place, a palace worked best, but any building with lots of rooms would do, and then you furnished it with whatever you wished to remember."

"You *furnished* it?" Marina shakes her head, perplexed.

"Ah, well, first you walked through the actual rooms and memorized their appearance. But once you had learned the rooms, in your imagination you could add anything you wish.

So, when we needed to memorize the Law of God, for instance, we closed our eyes and put a question and answer in each room."

Anya lowers her voice. "My school friend's family waited at the court," she continues. "Before the civil war, they had a beautiful house, thirty-five rooms. It is ministry offices now, but when I was a little girl, I used it for my memory palace. I can still tell you exactly what was in every one of those rooms." Anya stops, sets down her end of the divan, and closes her eyes. After a moment, her face softens.

"When one walks through the front doors, the entry has a marble floor and a very large Persian carpet. On the center of that carpet, where there is a rose design, I put the third question from the Law of God. 'What is necessary to please God and to save one's own soul?' Next, I go to the fireplace. It has a carved black marble mantel. Inside, instead of logs, I put the answer. 'In the first place, a knowledge of the true God and a right faith in him. In the second place, a life according to faith and good works.'" Anya opens her eyes. "I can walk through the entire house that way, stopping at each spot and putting there whatever I wish to remember. And later, I can come back and retrieve it all."

"This works?"

"I memorized the entire Law of God, all the Roman emperors and their reigns, and the Romanovs, too, of course. Everything. It's all still here." She taps her forehead. "I am like an old elephant. Ask me anything."

Marina is ready to get out of the car. She needs to use the toilet. When she asked, Helen said it was only a few more minutes to Andrei's, but Marina thinks they have been in the car longer than that. She leans forward and taps Dmitri on the shoulder. He twists around in the passenger seat. Strapped in like this, she can't reach his ear.

"Mnye nuzhno v tualyet," she whispers.

They have turned onto a long gravel road, and Marina sees a handsome gray clapboard house set into a stand of trees.

"We're here, Mama," Helen says. Cars line the road, but there is an open space in the driveway.

Marina sighs with relief when her son appears from behind the house and strides toward them across the lawn, his arms wide in greeting. He will take care of her.

"You're here," Andrei announces. "Good to see you, Helen." He gives his sister a big bear hug. "Heard you had an adventure getting here." Marina wonders what adventure Helen has had. She will have to remember to ask.

Andrei comes around the car, squeezes Dmitri, and finally leans in to help extricate her from the backseat.

"How's my best girl?"

He dips his head to hear her whispered request.

"Of course. Is this an emergency?" She nods.

"You two go ahead. Everyone's around back. We're running a little behind with the rehearsal, but tell Naureen to start without me."

He turns back to Marina and steers her across the lawn. "Are you ready for the big day tomorrow?"

She does a quick internal scan, but nothing surfaces. "I am," she says brightly. "Tomorrow comes, ready or not."

"That's the truth. It's been one thing after another around here. One of Katie's bridesmaids seems to have come down with food poisoning. And then this morning, the florist called. A shipment of flowers got left at the dock in Anacortes." They take the porch steps slowly.

"I should maybe go to get them?"

"The flowers? Oh, no, Naureen's on it. No, you just relax for now, Mama." At the top of the steps, he says, "You know the way, right? Through the living room, first door on the left?"

She nods.

"I better get down there. The kids are chomping at the bit. Come down to the beach when you're through."

The first room she walks into is cool and dark. Sunlight falls in gold slats through the shutters and stripes the floor. With its stone fireplace and exposed ceiling beams, the room reminds her of the old dachas and hunting lodges. She looks in the fireplace, but there is nothing there except the black husk of a log. In front of the fireplace is a couch with a bright red nylon sleeping bag on it. And here is a photograph of three smiling people. Andrei. His wife. Think. What is her name? Naureen.

Put her in the fireplace. Naureen. And a little girl with braces on her teeth.

Her bladder tugs insistently, reminding her that she has to use the toilet. Andrei told her through the living room, then . . . nothing. Well, just find it, she thinks. Here is the living room. Go through it.

Marina walks into the dining room and around into a spacious kitchen. Through the kitchen windows, she can see a lawn that falls softly away to water. A group of people is gathered down near the beach. Past the kitchen and a little laundry room is a stairway going up. Beyond the stairs, she is circling back onto a hallway with doors on either side. She opens each one. A bedroom. Another bedroom. A room with a television like a movie screen. Finally, and not a moment too soon, a toilet.

It is delightful to make water after holding it for so long. She listens to the music of water on water and feels the wonderful release inside her. And to sit where it is warm and private, not squatting over a chamber pot in the bitter cold. One of the effects of this deterioration seems to be that as the scope of her attention narrows, it also focuses like a magnifying glass on smaller pleasures that have escaped her notice for years. She keeps these observations to herself. She tried once to point out to Dmitri the bottomless beauty in her glass of tea. It looked like amber with buried embers of light, and when held just so, there was a rainbow in the glass that took her breath away. He nodded sympathetically but mostly looked concerned. What would he say if she told him her pee sounded like a symphony?

Yes, isn't it beautiful? This is called the Early Italian Renaissance Room, and is a fine example of the historicism style. Notice the fine gilded ornamentation on the ceiling and over the doors. The columns here are made of jasper, and these impressive doors are inlaid with precious woods and decorated with painted porcelain cameos.

If I could direct your attention over here, please. In all this splendor, she would be easy to miss, she is so small and quiet, but this is one of the treasures of the collection. She is exquisite, is she not? Such liquidity and grace. Simone Martini was the leading artist of the early fourteenth-century Siennese school, and his work is particularly rare. This little Madonna was once half of a folding diptych; the other wing, which has gone missing, portrayed the Angel Gabriel. So the modern viewer can see only part of the picture. To us, she appears to be lost in her own thoughts, her head tilted in dreamy contemplation. But actually she is listening to an unseen angel who is telling her that she will give birth to the son of God.

The first snows have come early this year. It is only October, but already there are fifty millimeters on the roof. On the radio, the snow is heralded as a good sign because it means winter is coming, and winter has always been Russia's salvation. It was the Russian winter that turned back Napoleon, and now, they say, it will keep Hitler out of Moscow.

The Nazis have turned their armies toward Moscow, and despite the suicidal bravery of the Red Army and the citizenry, they have been advancing inexorably, just as they did when they moved against Leningrad. But there are signs that the snow and slush are slowing their progress.

And on this front, the Germans have stopped moving entirely. It seems they have decided not to invade after all and to simply level Leningrad with bombs. Some days, there are as many as a dozen air raids. There are nights when Marina never leaves her post on the roof, and during the day, work has been interrupted so often that they have begun to ignore the sirens. The noise is deafening, but they work through it now, listening to the whine of shells and the thud of bombs and with one part of their brains calculating their distance.

This morning, though, is quiet. The interludes between

bombing raids are what stand out. It has begun to snow again, the flakes falling slowly outside the tall arched windows of the Early Italian Renaissance Room. Marina has never heard such a deep silence, only Anya's and her footsteps on the parquet floors.

Anya is helping Marina build a memory palace in the museum. "Someone must remember," Anya says, "or it all disappears without a trace, and then they can say it never was." So each morning, they get up early and the two women make their way slowly through the halls. They add a few more rooms each day, mentally restocking the Hermitage, painting by painting, statue by statue.

The old woman stops at an arched frame and swipes the edges with her feather duster. Marina has noticed that she is very careful to dust only the frame and not the space the painting itself would occupy. Marina pulls up behind her.

"A Madonna," Marina says, but her mind is a blank. "Just a minute, don't tell me."

It's a Madonna, but there must have been a hundred Madonnas in these rooms, and when Marina is tired and hungry, they start to blur into one another. She is always tired and hungry now, even just after eating.

Marina stares at the wall, but all she can see are women in enormous hoop skirts and self-satisfied gentlemen in powdered wigs. For some reason, the Early Italian Renaissance Room has become a temporary home for a dozen court portraits en route to the vaults. They have been left leaning against all the walls.

Think, she chides herself. Everything in the museum was displayed in strict order of chronology and provenance. So after the two Gerinis, early-fifteenth-century Florentine school, comes . . . what?

"Close your eyes," Anya says. "All you can see with your eyes open is the room as it is now."

Marina does as she is told.

"Now, go into your memory and pretend that you are leading a tour again. Walk into the room again."

She imagines walking into the room. She is leading a tour of dukes and duchesses, the figures from the court portraits. The Early Italian Renaissance Room, she informs them. In your day, you would have known it as the First Reception Room. You would have waited here to meet with the ambassador or members of the court. She can see the white stuccoed walls, intersected with paneled pilasters. The paintings are hung in a single row above the blue stone wainscot.

Sure enough, the paintings begin coming into focus in her mind: the crucifixions, the saints, the Madonna in her dark green robes and gilt halo.

"She's the one with the two saints and the little angels at her ears. Oh, what's her name?" Marina hesitates and then it comes in a rush. "*Madonna and Child with the Saints James the Less, John the Baptist and Angels*. Bicci di Lorenzo. Florentine school. I don't remember the dates."

Marina had thought this would be easier. After all, she has led tours of these rooms for two years, and she prided herself on having learned more of the collection than some guides who had worked there a decade. But she has quickly discovered how spotty her knowledge is. On the general museum tours, they skipped entire wings and walked groups through many of the rooms without stopping. Even on the specialized excursions through the picture gallery, they described only a few selected paintings in each room. In this room, for instance, they stopped only at the smallest painting in the room, Martini's *Madonna of the Annunciation*.

She has no trouble with the pieces that were on her tour scripts, but it is harder to remember the paintings in between, though she has passed them thousands of times. And then there are the countless vases and bibelots, and all the marble cupids and busts and torsos.

Anya, however, was a room attendant. She would spend an entire day sitting in one spot, and over the years, she seems to have committed the entire museum to memory. She can walk into a room, go to any spot on the wall, and describe for Marina what was there. She has no formal schooling in art and knows nothing about styles or schools or the individual provenances, sometimes not even the name of the artist or the work, but she knows what everything looked like. Her memory is limited only by what she couldn't see from her chair. For instance, in the Hall of Twenty Columns, where the numismatic collection was displayed, Anya can describe each vase on its pedestal and the placement around the hall of the various glass-fronted cases, but the contents of those cases might have been buttons or candies for all she knows. Otherwise, she is a marvel. Marina doubts that even Director Orbeli himself knows the contents of the museum as well as Anya does. In fact, she has wondered if perhaps she should tell Orbeli about Anya. Mightn't she be useful when the art comes home again, to speed up the rehanging?

When she brought this up with Uncle Viktor, though, he said, "I am sure Iosef Abgarovitch knows what is in his own museum, Marina, and doesn't need the help of one of the babushki."

"But isn't it amazing?" Marina persisted. She felt as though she had discovered a treasure, like Uncle Viktor must have felt when they found the first cuneiform at Karmir-Blur. "It's not just the important pieces she knows. We were walking down the 1812 Gallery yesterday and she described the faces of the generals." There are more than three hundred of these portraits, and to Marina they are indistinguishable, one from the next.

Viktor, though, wasn't particularly impressed. "It is a parlor trick, Marina. What is the use of this if she doesn't even know who they are?"

It is a good question, and Marina doesn't know how to answer it. She thinks that somehow it must matter, though, to see the art even if one doesn't know what it means.

The Leonardo Room is as hushed as a nursery. Here there are no frames, only the two freestanding panels that held Leonardo's Madonnas. Marina pauses at the first panel and recites. *"The Madonna and Child,* known also as the Benois Madonna, by Leonardo da Vinci. An early work of Leonardo's, one of two Madonnas begun by him in Florence in 1478. This is one of the few undisputed originals by the master."

Of all the Madonnas in the museum, Marina could never forget this one. She loved this mother and child and misses the two of them with a particular ache. The Mary is completely human, not a remote beauty but a young girl delighted with the surprise of this child, and the Christ Child is so fat and dimpled, a fleshy baby like Mikhail when he was younger. He perches on little Mary's lap, his pudgy fingers grasping at the flower she holds up to his gaze and studying it as a scientist might. Secretly, she thinks of this painting as hers. With Mary's high forehead, they even resemble each other, and Marina has sometimes fantasized that she herself could be the model.

"Such a mess. Do you see this?" Anya is standing in front of the other panel, the one that held the second Leonardo Madonna. She shakes her head and clucks, pointing to the floor at her feet. Sand has drifted or been tracked from the corner, where it is heaped on a tarpaulin. "This will scratch the varnish."

She points across the room to where a push broom has been left leaning in the doorway. "Get me that, would you, dear?"

Marina walks across the parquet and fetches the broom. When she turns around, the old woman is kneeling in front of the panel like a penitent before an altar, her head bowed, her skirt pooled on the floor.

She sees Marina watching her and says, "I will say a prayer for you, too."

"I'm not a believer," Marina objects.

The old woman appraises her. "Everyone believes in something." Then she smiles and says, "But you mean that you are too educated to believe in the superstitious nonsense of old people. Yes?" She waits for Marina to answer, but the girl is polite and says nothing.

"Then my prayer will do you no harm."

With a practiced gesture, the old woman touches her fingers to her forehead, her belly, and each of her shoulders and begins mumbling to herself. Marina averts her eyes, with the same embarrassment she feels when she witnesses the spastic fumbling of cripples or the ranting of the feebleminded. She wonders if she should leave Anya alone, but this, too, seems rude, and so she waits, leaning on the broom and studying the blank wall to which Anya is praying.

Out of the shadowy square of paneling that marks where

the painting once hung, the Litta Madonna materializes. With her aquiline nose and porcelain features, the Madonna is the perfect study of contentment, gazing down at her nursing child. The Christ Child, though, is the center of the painting. He is not a blank lump of sweet pink flesh but already commands an adult presence. With one hand, he grasps the exposed breast and suckles absently, his dark, shadowy eyes gazing out of the painting, sizing up the scene before him, an elderly Soviet cleaning woman kneeling at his feet. He looks unsurprised.

When Anya has finished her prayers, she crosses herself again, smooths her skirt flat, and tells Marina to sweep the sand over the hem. The old woman licks her fingers and gathers up stray grains. Marina tucks the feather duster under her arm and helps the old woman clamber back onto her feet with her skirt full of sand. Before they leave, Anya presses her lips to the Christ Child's toes and mumbles something to him. At the door, Marina glances back over her shoulder and sees the Christ Child still watching them guardedly. And then he spits the nipple from his mouth and burps.

We are both insane, she thinks.

She knows that her visions are easily explained by exhaustion. By hunger. By all the stresses of living like cattle. But they are also a necessary illusion, a gift.

Past a billowing white tent, the wedding party, some twenty people, is gathered down at the beach, where a regiment of folding chairs faces a rented arbor, and beyond that, the sheltered waters of Pillikut Bay.

"Hello!" A professionally cheerful woman accosts Helen and Dmitri as they cross the lawn. "I'm Sandy Holcomb, the wedding planner. And you are . . . ?"

"Dmitri Buriakov and Helen Webb," Helen says.

The wedding planner brightens and exclaims, "Wonderful. We're just about to get started. Would you mind sitting here and letting us know if you can hear everyone?"

"A wedding planner?" Dmitri says to Helen. "Have you ever heard of such a thing?"

While the wedding planner walks everyone through their paces, Helen and Dmitri sit in the back row, standing in for the guests who will assemble for the ceremony tomorrow. It is like watching a community theater rehearsal. As the groom's brother and two friends escort the mothers across the lawn, they undermine each other's weak attempts at solemnity with self-conscious grins. The young man escorting the mother of the bride whispers something in her ear. It's possible, Helen

81

thinks, that he might be flirting with her. Naureen is only a few years younger than Helen, but she is tanned and athletic, one of those lean Katharine Hepburn types who seem to age like hardwood.

Helen remembers how surprised they all were when Andrei, at age thirty-six, turned up with Naureen. He had seemed so destined to remain a bachelor. Helen can't recall his ever bringing a girl home before or showing any interest in one. Though her own girlfriends were always turning coy and flirty when they first met him, he was hopelessly serious and woodenly indifferent to their charms, a nerd who seemed content to bury himself in his textbooks.

Later, his life had revolved around his practice, and a specialty in corneal transplants meant that his schedule was more or less dictated by the randomness of car accidents. He moved away from home only to purchase a condo within walking distance of the hospital. Helen went there once or twice, and all you needed to know about Andrei's private life then could be read in those sparsely furnished rooms: takeout containers on the kitchen counter, a dead cactus on the windowsill, empty dry-cleaning bags draped over a bar stool. He'd brought his maple bedroom set from home, and the nightstand was piled with medical journals, the headboard stuck with threaded needles. When Helen asked, he explained that at night, he lay in bed and practiced threading needles in the dark, so he would be able to do it in surgery while wearing magnifying goggles. "The magnification is so high, everything blurs. It's like being blind," he had said, apparently without irony.

Helen guesses he probably never had a date in his life that wasn't set up by someone else. So when her parents called her in Phoenix and said that Andrei had met a girl and it looked serious, Helen pegged her as an exceptionally determined husband-hunter with her cap set for a surgeon. When Naureen turned out to be pretty and ten years his junior to boot, that sealed it in Helen's eyes. She wasn't particularly close to her brother, but she didn't like to see him get snookered, either.

That was twenty-five years ago, and Helen freely admits she misjudged. Naureen's the best thing that could have happened to Andrei, giving him a home and a life that he never would have come up with on his own. Under her care, he has even developed a few outside interests and can hold up his end of a conversation about restaurants or politics or local sports. Last year, she bought him a titanium fly rod and lessons. "I'm working him up to hobbies," she joked. "He's going to have to retire at some point, and I can't have him hanging around the house all day." She seems to adore Andrei, and he, in turn, visibly softens in her presence, his careful self-possession melting in spaniel-like gratitude when she praises him or takes his arm. If it's all for show, Helen has never been able to spot a crack in the facade. They really do seem to be in love, even all these years later.

Behind Naureen comes a girl who looks to be about five and is the niece of the groom. She processes with resolute concentration, determinedly flinging imaginary handfuls of petals from her wicker basket. Her younger brother stops stone-still just short of the chairs and eyes the assembled group with undisguised suspicion. The laughter that erupts humiliates him, and he veers unsteadily back toward his mother. It requires a good deal of coaching to lure him back down the aisle.

"Okay, group," chirps the wedding organizer, "let's just get through this and then we can all relax and have fun." One look at her tells that spontaneous fun is not her forte.

"Bridesmaids, take your time. Wait five counts before the next girl. That's right." A redhead dressed in shorts and black satin shoes takes slow, halting steps across the lawn, gripping an imaginary bouquet and looking as though she may topple off her heels at every step.

"Now we'll leave a little space for our absent bridesmaid. How is she feeling? Well, one way or the other, the musicians will just keep playing until everyone is down the aisle. And then the sister." After a gap comes Jen, the groom's sister.

"Now, wait ten counts. The music will change to the wedding march."

"No," Naureen says. "They're playing *Ode to Joy*."

"Okay, so wait for the change. And here it is." She raises her hand. "Katie, Mr. Buriakov."

As Katie and Andrei approach the beach at a measured pace, Dmitri rises and Helen follows suit, the stand-in guests. The bride-to-be glides across the uneven lawn, one hand holding a bouquet constructed of ribbons and tissue paper flowers glued to a doily-encrusted paper plate, the other hand resting lightly on her father's arm. Even dressed in a T-shirt and jeans, she looks radiant. She has an expression that Helen has sometimes seen on brides and new mothers but didn't experience herself: a calm, clear-eyed gaze that takes in the world just as it is and pronounces it good.

The rehearsal drones forward, and Helen lapses into memories of her own wedding. Anyone with the dullest intuition could have foretold the future in the dregs of that day. When she arrived at the church with her parents, Don had been standing outside the entrance, smoking a cigarette. Marina had tried to shoo him off, saying it was bad luck to see the bride before the ceremony, but Don had just said, "I think we've already had our bad luck."

Dmitri keeps glancing back at the house, and finally he whispers, "I'm going to go find your mother." He's about to stand up, but Helen puts her hand over his.

"Is something wrong, Papa?"

"It's nothing for you to worry about." When he sees that this is exactly the response guaranteed to make her worry, he amends his answer. "Your mother, she doesn't like to confess her limits, but she needs looking after a little. That's all. Your brother makes too much of this," he adds. "You know how he is."

Of course she does. Helen squeezes her father's hand. "You sit. I'll get her."

Inside the house, Helen calls her mother. She taps on the closed bathroom door. "Mama? Are you okay?"

After a moment, the toilet flushes and her mother emerges.

"You're missing the show," Helen says.

"Am I?"

"No, not really. They're just walking through the ceremony. Actually, I just came up to see if you were okay."

"Okay?"

Her mother looks a little puzzled, and Helen is conscious of how idiotic she must sound.

"I don't know what it is about weddings. I'm always expecting disaster. You remember my wedding?"

Marina nods. "You were a beautiful bride."

Helen rolls her eyes. "Mama, I was such a mess, you were ready to call the whole thing off. Don't you remember that?"

Helen has never forgotten. Standing in the little room off the chapel, she was crying and her mother had turned to her and said that it wasn't too late, they could still send everyone home. She couldn't have stunned Helen more if she had sprouted a third eye.

"I remember," Marina says. "I didn't say this because you were a mess. I said this because you didn't need this boy. Babies need only their mother's milk and clean diapers." Her voice is matter-of-fact, practical.

Helen is amazed all over again. At the time, she had dismissed the offer out of hand. It was 1970 and, at least in Seattle, having a baby out of wedlock was still an unthinkable shame. She'd had neither the imagination nor the courage to envision an alternative to marriage, even, or especially, when the alternative was proposed by her mother.

Now she wants to ask this sweet little old lady in her ruffled blouse and sensible flats, Who are you, anyway?

Even in her sleep, Marina hears the air-raid sirens. In the bowels of the Hermitage, the shriek of the sirens above are muted, but she is like a mother attuned to the cries of her infant. This must be what it is like to be a mother, she thinks, this endless exhaustion, days and nights measured by the wails of a baby. But like a good mother, though she curses to herself, she gets up, grabs her binoculars and sheepskin, and climbs up the steps toward her post. It is time for her shift.

In order to get to the roof, she must first cross through the Hall of Twenty Columns. At night, the hall is black and utterly terrifying. Because there are no blackout curtains, lights are prohibited, and only one tiny bulb winks like a distant star at the base of the far doorway.

She pauses briefly at the entrance and catches her breath, tries to slow her pounding heart. It seems a silly fear in light of all the very real terrors, but this passage frightens her.

She steps gingerly into the void and tries for a few steps to take the direct route down the center of the hall. It is too much, though, floating unmoored in the blackness. She backs up until her hands find a wall, and then works her way along this wall, step by step, hugging the edge of the room. The columns cut her off from the tiny guide light, but it is still marginally better than the dizziness of open space.

It is so dark that she cannot see even her own hands, can only feel the walls and hear her footsteps echo on the mosaic floor. This is what it might be like to be blind. The dark is not solid, though. It is layered with shades of black. Huge shapes loom suddenly out of shadow. The columns, she reminds herself.

Deep into the huge room, she feels the still air around her shift, and something hovering at the edge of her vision. She thinks she hears the whisper of her name.

"Hello?" Her voice comes out low and hoarse. She listens hard, past the pounding of her heart in her ears, past the shrieking siren outside. Nothing. Taking another step forward, she hears her footfall and what is either its echo or another person's step in the hall. "Is someone here?" The sense of another presence, though unattached to any physical cues, is unshakable. She has an animal's sense of being watched.

If she doesn't keep moving, she will be unable to go on. She reminds herself that she has a duty upstairs, and then she closes her eyes and forces her feet forward steadily, her hands groping the wall. She begins to sing, loudly, a stout song about the victorious People's Army that has been playing relentlessly on the loudspeakers during the day and on the radio every night before sign-off. *Brothers fighting side by side/Marching toward the vision we can see/Though bloodied and weary, the turning of the tide/Will lead us unbowed to victory.* Halfway through a breathless second chorus, the guide bulb winks into view again and she dashes gratefully to the doorway.

The wind off the river blows drifts of icy snow across the Hermitage roof, a desolate steppe. When she climbs onto the platform, she sits down and pulls the sheepskin closer around her.

Aside from the sirens, it is quiet tonight, no planes yet. But the moon is rising, so they will come. She hates the moon. It is dead, and its flat, dead light draws in Fascist planes like moths. Though she knows her perspective has been poisoned by the war, it is hard to see why poets make such a romantic fuss over an ugly, pockmarked disk.

She buries her face in the fleece, feeling the pull of sleep threatening to swallow her. Most gather in pairs so they can keep each other awake and pass the night by talking, but Olga Markhaeva is ill. She has the dysentery that has been plaguing so many of the staff. Marina has been covering for her for the past several nights so she will not lose her worker's rations. When Marina radios downstairs, she pretends that Olga is up here with her. She suspects that Sergei Pavlovich is not fooled, that in fact he is conspiring with her to protect Olga, but he says nothing.

To keep herself awake, she practices her memory palace. Walking the actual rooms by day is no longer the challenge it was. In some of the rooms, the empty frames provide a map, and all she has to do is fill inside the frames. But at night, she must work entirely from memory. Tonight she imagines herself in the Rembrandt Room, starting at the east entrance. She closes her eyes and puts herself in the doorway. She takes in the green walls, the marble wainscoting, the solemnity of the room peopled with quiet Dutch faces and figures, and then she begins to conjure up the first painting she would see.

It is Ferdinand Bol's *Old Woman with a Book*, a severe-looking shrew in widow's weeds, clutching an open Bible in her lap. Her husband provided for her well, one can tell from the big brooch on her chest, but her expression suggests that she will make her heirs grovel and then leave it all to the church.

Across from her is *Flora,* a portrait of Rembrandt's young wife, Saskia, painted in the first year of their marriage. Saskia's moon face is hardly that of the goddess of spring, but the newlywed Rembrandt was so clearly smitten with her that she reflects his happiness. She is dressed in rich finery, silks and embroidery, and to suggest that she is the goddess of spring, her headdress is a lavish Baroque bouquet of flowers. A tulip hangs like a bell over her left ear. In one hand, she holds a staff similarly bedecked with flowers, and her other hand rests on what looks at first to be her pregnant belly. The mounded bodice is merely the fashion of the time, but Marina imagines that Saskia is dreaming a baby into existence, her gaze is so inward and still.

Next to Saskia, Rembrandt's scholar looks up from his writing and appears dumbfounded by the scene he faces. When one turns around to follow his gaze, there she is, a lounging nude taking up the entire wall. The nude seems at first to be shielding her eyes from the scorn of Bol's sour-faced old woman, but no, she is looking at someone else.

This is the painter's first full-size female nude. It illustrates the myth of Danae, a beautiful princess whose father, the king, locked her away in a bronze tower to thwart potential suitors. There she is visited by Zeus, who has admired her. As is his habit when he wishes to satisfy his passions, he transmogrifies himself—with the beautiful Leda, he became a swan, with Europa, a white bull, with Antiope, a satyr, and so on— but with Danae he takes form as a shower of gold. Here Danae is shielding her face from his light, or perhaps she is reaching out to him; it is tantalizingly hard to tell. But tonight her life will change. He will impregnate her, and in time she will give birth to a god, Perseus.

And there is *The Sacrifice of Isaac*. Very dramatic, Isaac's body limp and glowing. His face is covered by Abraham's hand.

Portrait of an Old Jew. Brown. An old face. Old hands.

David and Uriah. The red robes. The scribe in the background.

The Holy Family. Mother. Baby.

The Return of

The Return of

The light dims, and the quiet browns and golds of Rembrandt's people recede into the dark. Slowly, the room falls away beneath her, and she is lifting up into the sky, flying.

It is like a beautiful, disturbing dream. She is almost in the clouds, and the moon drifts in, drifts out, silvering the ghostly city below. She can see the roof of the Winter Palace, then past the rows of copper statues that line its perimeter, past church spires engraved on the black sky, past the pale dome of St. Isaac's. Below her, the frozen Neva glitters and weaves. Above her, the blimps hover silently in the clouds. During the day, they are ugly sausages. But at night they swim like enormous white whales through a dark sea.

She is swimming with the whales. She hears what sounds like the rhythmic whoosh of their breath. And then someone is beside her, breathing hotly in her ear, stroking her belly and the insides of her thighs, pulling her along through the air. Marina. The voice whispers her name. Marina. Come to me.

She starts, hearing the drone of distant planes. Who knows how long she has been here, an hour, perhaps two, she cannot read her wristwatch.

She finds her radio and switches it on.

"Hello?" She is trembling, but not with cold. Her body feels liquid and warm. "Sergei Pavlovich, this is the North Platform. I'm standing by. Over."

She pulls her binoculars from their case and lifts them to her eyes. In the distance, she finds the approaching silhouettes of planes. As she sweeps the binoculars back toward the embankment, her view suddenly fills with an enormous silhouette. Inexplicably, one of the statues from the roof of the Winter Palace has transported itself several hundred meters north onto the barren roof of the New Hermitage building. The statue, a naked god, gleams in the moonlight, poised at the edge of the roof, so close to the brink that from this angle it appears to be floating suspended over the river.

She is transfixed. As she watches, the statue slowly turns in her direction. He is shockingly beautiful and blindingly bright. She lifts her hand to shield her eyes from the light.

"Oh my god." Although her voice seems to disappear in the wind, the statue smiles at her and stretches his arm out to her, beckoning. Her chest tightens. She feels a shock of recognition, as in a dream when suddenly one knows, knows with an unshakable certainty, no matter that it should be impossible.

"What is it? Marina?" It is Sergei's voice. The radio. She can barely lift it to her mouth.

"There is a . . ." she begins, but her voice falters. "A man." She is not speaking loudly enough to be heard. She gasps in air.

"Someone is up here," she says. She refrains from mentioning that he is naked.

"I don't understand. Do you mean Olga Markhaeva?"

"No," she breathes. Her heart is pounding wildly. Every-thing is gold, light, hot. She closes her eyes against the light and the radio falls from her hand. She feels herself lifting up into the night on a slow, throbbing pulse, and she lets herself be carried off on it.

Her skin sparks to a touch sliding down her throat, circling first one nipple, then the other, each touch sending streaks of electric current coursing through her. The long, agonizing stretch of her belly, and then the wet, satiny folds between her thighs. She feels the heat radiating from him expand inside her, and she is frantic, rocking back and forth, back and forth, wildly climbing a series of molten waves. The beat of wings quickens, crescendos into a roar, and she is turned inside out with a flash of heat. Warm milk courses through her limbs and leaks out between her legs.

It is like being underwater, rising toward the light and hearing muffled voices above the surface.

"Look. Do you see the eagle, Marina?"

"We got seats right behind home plate, five rows back. You could see the guys spit."

"Do you see it?"

"How'd you score those?"

"Oh, Jen's got some clients. They've been real pains. I guess they wanted to make it up to her."

Marina is sitting in a comfortable chair on the patio with her daughter-in-law. She knows time has passed and those around her have continued on in this world without her, conversing and drinking.

It is beautiful here. The sun is hanging just above the horizon, streaking the sky with long shreds of purple and orange, fringing the woods in velvety shadow. Behind her, music drifts out the open windows, and at regular intervals a tinny sequence of arcade bleeps and hoots announces that one of the kids has scored on the computer upstairs.

Everyone is looking up, and Naureen points out to Marina

a dark silhouette gliding on air currents, its wings spread like ragged fingers.

"Aren't birds wonderful?" Marina says.

"It's one of the things I love about coming up here," Naureen agrees. "There's a nesting pair on White Point, and we see them nearly every day."

"A pair of bluebirds made a nest in our hanging basket," Marina says. "There were two eggs, but one of the chicks didn't survive. The mother and father bird tended it for weeks, and then one day the little bird flew away and that was the last time we saw it."

They are silent for a moment, watching the eagle.

"Aren't birds wonderful?"

"Yes."

"A pair of bluebirds made a nest in our hanging basket."

"Marina, are you through with that? You hardly touched it."

Marina looks down at a bowl of melting ice cream. It looks something like blockade jelly.

"Marina?"

"Maybe I will have a bite more."

"I could get you some more. That's all melted."

"No, it's just the way I like it, dear." She eats a spoonful just to confirm this. "We ate a jelly made from joiner's glue."

"What?"

"Joiner's glue. You use it to glue the picture frames."

"You ate glue?" Naureen looks puzzled. Marina wonders if she has used the wrong word. Glue. Glue. It sounds wrong somehow.

"Glue, to stick things together? It was made from sinews of

95

beef, I think. We melted it down. It was pretty tasty, I remember."

"Dear god," Naureen breathes. "This was during the war?"

"Yes, dear." Marina smiles. "We didn't eat it before. It wasn't *that* good."

"I can't imagine. The war, I mean."

"No, it was not imaginable . . ."

People crowd in on Marina. A swirl of faces and bodies: the naked women in the public bath, women with blackened legs wavering in the steamy light, Olga Markhaeva calling out the locations of fires, the swaddled gray mass of humanity on the streets, moving like ghosts. An emaciated woman has fallen in the snow, a scarecrow with hollow eyes who stretches a claw up toward her. Marina's eyes are watering, and she shakes her head roughly.

"Are you all right, Marina?"

Marina reaches for Naureen's hand and grips it tightly in her own. More distressing than the loss of words is the way that time contracts and fractures and drops her in unexpected places.

"I didn't mean to upset you," Naureen says. She scoots her chair closer to Marina and with her free hand rubs the back of Marina's hand.

It's like a terrible thaw. Like the Hermitage that spring when all the snow on the roof melted. For weeks, they bailed water, carried buckets of filthy water out into the courtyard. Water leaked from out of the walls, through the roof. It ran down the Jordan staircase like a stream. And it just kept coming and coming.

Marina takes a slow breath. "I am becoming like the museum. Everything, it is leaking. It is horrible."

Naureen doesn't pursue this. She continues to stroke

Marina's hand, and the two sit quietly. After a few minutes, Naureen changes the subject. "Tell me about Andrei when he was a baby."

Marina brightens a little at the mention of her son. "Oh, my. When I delivered him, the nurses were astonished. The babies born during the blockade were runty things mostly, tiny and deformed or born dead. But not Andrei—he weighed over three kilos and he was perfect. He never cried. Not even during bombing raids. The shells were so loud, like devils shrieking, but he would be in his blanket, half asleep. His face was so calm. I would check him every few minutes—I was afraid he stopped breathing. I wondered even if he was born deaf. But he was an unusual child. People would stop me in the street to admire him. He had a head of golden curls just like his father."

"Dmitri had blond hair?"

Marina shakes her head impatiently. "Not Dima. He isn't a god, dear."

Naureen smiles. "No, I guess he isn't. None of them are, are they?"

The Rembrandt Room. At first, it seems empty, the room is so quiet and dark. The walls are a soft green, the color of faded billiards felt, and the flat ceiling is simply decorated. A series of half walls divides the room, so that one cannot see right away that it is actually full of people. They are quiet, contemplative people, old men in ruffs and modest young women lost in their own thoughts.

Beckoning from the far end of the room is a startling figure, Danae. She is an odalisque, a nude lying in repose, seductive, awaiting her lover. It is a classic pose, but Rembrandt in his genius has painted an ordinary woman, lush of body but not idealized. Her belly is full and spills onto the bed. Her face is almost plain but transformed by wonder.

Everything in the painting is luxuriant and, aptly, golden: the roundness of her heavy belly and delicate breasts, the soft, pale curves of her hip and thigh. The lavish boudoir is draped with heavy brocades and velvets and fine linens, and Danae, though she is nude, is adorned with coral bracelets. She stretches out full length on her bed, propped up on one elbow, with her other hand raised in awe or greeting toward her miraculous visitor. Zeus's presence is obscured in drapery, but she is bathed in his radiant light. She sees the miracle, what the viewer cannot see. Behind her and half-hidden by drapery stands her elderly guard. She, too, looks on in amazement.

It is late. Most of the wedding party has gone back to the inn, but Helen has lingered. Naureen is gathering up the last of the wineglasses and plates left on tables outside, and Andrei is folding up the extra chairs and stowing them against the side of the house.

Helen studies the bottom of her wineglass. "Why didn't you tell me she's got Alzheimer's?"

Andrei picks up another chair and adds it to the sheaf under the eaves. "We don't know for certain that it's Alzheimer's. She's got symptoms of dementia, but that's not at all uncommon in people her age. It's not my field, but I don't think even a good gerontologist can diagnose it with complete accuracy."

"Oh, for god's sake, Andrei," Helen snaps. "I wasn't asking for a diagnosis. I'm just saying that you might have mentioned to me that our mother is losing her mind."

Andrei stiffens, but before he can respond, Naureen shoots him a look. "We should have prepared you, Helen," she says. She blows out a votive candle and sits down. "It's been such a gradual thing, I guess we all kind of take it in stride, but it must be pretty upsetting if you haven't seen her for a while."

"I don't think she knew who I was." Helen presses a finger

100

against one tear duct, then the other. "When I came to pick them up, she invited me in and asked about my family. The way she said it, it was like I was a stranger."

Naureen gives her husband another look, a visual nudge, and he joins them at the table.

"She's just a little absent sometimes. I'm sure she knew who you were," Andrei offers.

"And what makes you so sure about that?" Helen's voice is arch.

He takes a deep breath and visibly composes himself. "You're right. I don't know anything for sure. They both play their cards pretty close to the chest."

"Tell me about it."

"Papa won't even talk about it. He pretends like she's fine. But you can see why I've been pushing to get them moved. They're doing okay now, but it's good to have things in place."

It is so quiet that they can hear the patter of moths batting against the porch light, the metallic pinging of a boat's halyard in the bay.

Helen pours herself another swig of wine. "Has she ever said anything to you about living in a cellar in Russia?"

"What are you talking about?" Andrei asks.

"She mentioned some cousins, the family she lived with, and she said they all lived in a cellar. You don't remember anything like that?"

"That was before my time."

"No, I know, but she never said anything to you about a cellar?"

"No."

"Don't you wonder?"

101

"Wonder what?"

"Why we don't know. Isn't it weird that we don't know anything about them?" Maybe it's the wine or the lack of sleep, because she feels she's being very clear and yet her brother doesn't seem to get it. "She said they lived in a cellar with hundreds of people."

"Helen," Naureen says, "I don't know how much credence you want to give to everything she says. Tonight, we were talking and one minute she seemed fine, and then next thing you know, she's telling me how she used to eat glue and swim with whales. Oh, and she met Zeus."

"Who?" Andrei asks.

"Zeus. The Greek god."

"Maybe she knew someone named Zeus."

"She said he was a god, Andrei. She also said he was your real father."

"Zeus? She said Zeus was my father?" Andrei chuckles and shakes his head.

"Well, that makes perfect sense." Helen smiles in spite of herself. "She's always thought you were God's gift. Now we know why."

The two women laugh until they cry, and Andrei grins good-naturedly. "Yeah, yeah, very funny," he says, and they crack up again.

"Tell her about the recliner," Naureen urges.

"Well, for their anniversary, I bought them two new recliners. To replace those ratty old things they have in the living room. I could tell Papa liked them, but she kept at me until I sent them back. You know how she gets. Everything is more than she needs. I said, 'Don't you like them?' And she said,

'They're lovely, but you should save your money. Buy yourself a lamb chop.'"

"A lamb chop?" Helen is poised for the explanation.

Andrei shrugs. "Who knows. She mixes up words."

"Poor Papa."

"I guess. To hear him tell it, though, everything's just fine. You should see him. He's learned how to cook. He makes a real mean *shchi*." This is their mother's cabbage soup, a wonderful concoction with prunes and peppers and carrots. Helen can almost smell the pungent aroma of it that used to steam up the kitchen windows on winter afternoons.

"Remember how she used to make us wipe down our soup bowls with bread?" Helen asks.

Andrei grins. "You should have seen her, Naureen. She'd go nuts if we left anything on our plates. I mean anything. We had to stay at the table until they were clean. When I was a kid, I fell asleep face-first in a plate of Brussels sprouts. Oh, and remember the rhubarb?"

Helen rolls her eyes. "Stewed rhubarb. Canned rhubarb. Rhubarb juice. Chicken stuffed with rhubarb."

"Your birthday?" Andrei prompts. The two of them sputter with laughter and Helen adds the punch line. "Rhubarb spice cake!"

"Papa put in some rhubarb one year," she explains to Naureen. "The stuff went wild, it took over the whole garden. But she wasn't going to let any of it go to waste. It was like a religion with her."

"Eat until you see the pattern on the plate so tomorrow we will have nice weather," Andrei recites, imitating his mother's accent, and they convulse into laughter again.

Helen catches at her breath and releases a long, pent-up sigh.

"She just shoveled the food down us. I was such a fat kid, and then when I was in college and I started trying to diet, you'd have thought I was torturing her.

"I still can't throw out food. Last week, I was making a recipe that called for egg whites, and I had these yolks. Two lousy egg yolks, and I couldn't just dump them down the drain. It was like she was standing at my back, watching me. They're still in the fridge. All these little containers of leftovers. A cup of rice pilaf. Half an orange in plastic wrap. A half-dozen grapes shriveled like peas." She throws up her hands in mock surrender. "I've actually been thinking about getting another dog, just to have someone to feed the scraps to."

Seventy-five grams of bread. Bread that is half sawdust, a small, dense block. It is the size of a ticket stub in her palm, the weight of dead leaves. Many evenings, this is their only food, and they must eat very slowly to stretch out this morsel of black bread into the length of a meal. She pulls off a tiny corner. It is nearly tasteless, but Marina eats it slowly, focusing on the sensations of chewing and swallowing. She calls up in her imagination the flavors of foods she has eaten, sausages and watermelon and pickled beets.

Her uncle is reading aloud from the text of his upcoming lecture, a droning recitation of dates and numbers.

Monday, bread rations were cut again, down to two hundred and fifty grams a day for workers, half that for dependents like Aunt Nadezhda. Not even an infant could survive on such a meager portion, and this must be divided into three meals. Some people gobble up their entire day's ration as soon as they get it, but, as Uncle Viktor points out, they are fools. When the bread is gone, they are still hungry. There is never enough food to still one's hunger. But time, time is measured in the space between one meal and the next, and without bread to look forward to, the day never ends.

People are starving. They have been reduced to eating unimaginable things. Bubi, Mikhail's cat, was an early victim of their hunger. Not that they actually ate Bubi—they were still too squeamish for that—but they traded him away for a sack of potatoes and some cooking oil, knowing full well the fate to which they were consigning him. Now, they would eat him themselves without a second thought. They eat wallpaper paste and glue and even wood, and still they starve. The mind reels. It is unimaginable that in 1941, in Leningrad no less, people could actually be dying of starvation, and not just drunkards or ne'er-do-wells, but distinguished scholars and respected artists. Unimaginable, but true. They lie down and die as simply as going to sleep, and those left behind try to explain their deaths, try to find patterns to numb the horror. This person was elderly or that person was always thin as a matchstick. Those without purpose die sooner, and men are more susceptible than women, having less fat. Living alone is a liability, and having to share rations with dependents is a liability also.

Viktor has applied scientific rigor to the business of keeping them alive. In the mornings, he distributes the breakfast ration with the solemnity of a priest bestowing communion wafers. Later, when Nadezhda returns from the bakery with the bread, he carefully cuts it up into nine portions for that day's lunch and dinner and the following day's breakfast. Because Marina is doing physical labor and thus has higher caloric needs, her three nuggets of bread are cut slightly larger. They are wrapped in a cloth and set out of sight. On the days when the canteen serves up extra rations at lunch, a porridge made of boiled buckwheat groats or their famous aspic, the evening ration is halved again and the remainder set aside. If there is extra bread, he barters it on strict principles of nutrition and economy rather than succumbing, as Nadezhda might, to the temptations of the palate.

His scientific system of household management doesn't factor in luck, though, and Marina has come to suspect that their survival may depend on something beyond the bounds of reason—call it luck or miracles or whatever you wish. Since that day back in October when she saw Anya praying to the Benois Madonna, she has begun to petition the Madonnas as well. When they are making their morning rounds and pass a frame that held a Madonna, she furtively mumbles a quick prayer and then improvises something like the crossing gestures Anya made over her chest. She doesn't know the incantations one is supposed to recite. The first time, she just whispered, Help. Help us, please. That night, the god came to her on the roof.

Now she asks for things. She asks for Dmitri to come home. She asks for the god on the roof to return. She asks for food. It is foolish, a kind of wishing game that Mikhail and Tatiana might play.

Dmitri has not come home; neither has she heard any word of him. His division was decimated at Chudovo, and those who survived joined other divisions. He might be anywhere. Every morning, she scans the casualty list posted in the warden's room, looking for his name. When it isn't there, she feels a flush of gratitude. He may yet be alive, and who knows, perhaps Viktor will hear something of him when he goes to the front.

As for the god on the roof, she knows she imagined that. She has heard others complain of hallucinations brought on by hunger. Though this visitation felt more real than any moment before or since, a tangible consummation of the flesh, she must concede that there is no evidence to support such a wild rent in the fabric of the universe. She does not care. She has gone up to the roof night after night, hoping to hallucinate again, to be swept up into passion. But the statues on the roof have remained inanimate copper, refusing to alchemize into gold.

Still, there have been the miracles of food.

A week after Marina first approached the Madonnas, Nadezhda's china, which had been languishing in a consignment shop since July, miraculously sold. Viktor returned from the black market with rice and rusks, and the smoky rock candy made from molten sugar excavated from the charred basement of the Badayev warehouse. They were able to save their ration coupons for the rest of the month. Then two weeks ago, when there was nothing left, when Marina had begun fainting at the slightest exertion, a group of sailors on the Palace Embankment presented her with an armful of pine branches. She ate an entire branch on the way back to the shelter, gnawing on the bark. It tasted wonderful, sharp and spicy, like eating the forest. They heard that in the hospital the needles are boiled to extract vitamins for those with scurvy, so Nadezhda made a fragrant broth with the rest.

Now, though he would not call it luck, Viktor has secured a place with the Goodwill Delegation from the Hermitage that will visit the front tomorrow. For the entertainment of the troops, he is scheduled to deliver a lecture on the ancient civilization of Urartu. There will be a banquet following the proceedings, and an honorarium will be paid in butter and vodka.

Tonight, though, there is only bread. Marina disciplines herself to wait until Uncle Viktor finishes a page and has thumbed to the next sheet before she allows herself another nibble. Between bites, she tries to train her mind away from the bread and back to the lecture. She and Nadezhda are a test audience, charged with the thankless task of responding as they imagine a real audience of soldiers might. Before he began to read, Viktor suggested that they pretend they know nothing about Urartian culture.

"Understand that this was originally composed with a scholarly reader in mind. While I believe I've adjusted the text of my manuscript sufficiently to accommodate a general audience, there may be references here and there that need further elucidation. Naturally, I'm receptive to any suggestions."

This last part is not precisely true. Earlier, Marina made the mistake of offering a small suggestion about a turn of phrase that seemed unnecessarily stilted to her and might be improved by the substitution of the word *begin* for *commence*. Viktor treated her to a long discourse defending the propriety of his wording, noting that *commence* had a tone more suitable to the solemnity of the occasion.

"One might *begin* doing a household chore," he intoned, "but we are not talking about laundry here but rather the excavation of a culture."

And then he started the lecture over from the beginning.

The story of Urartu might be told as a compelling mystery story. There once was a powerful kingdom that ruled over the Caucasus for three centuries and then vanished completely from history. Only in the last few decades has it been rescued from oblivion, its temples and fortresses unearthed, its language transcribed, an entire culture that was buried for twenty-five centuries brought back to the surface.

However, Viktor's description drains the excitement from his subject, substituting detailed exposition of the digs and a painstaking analysis of sociological formation. Some of the leadenness is due, no doubt, to the scientific rigor of his discipline. The rest could be attributed to political necessity. Viktor Alekseevich Krasnov's version of Urartian culture is dutifully and remarkably prescient of Marx. In this, Marina thinks, his writing is no different from any other piece of writing for public consumption. There is rarely an original thought that isn't smothered under the deadening weight of Marxist theory. Take the museum guides' official tour script. If visitors had to navigate the picture gallery upstairs with only this document, they would quickly get lost. This script, which Marina and the other guides have memorized and recite verbatim, translates an innocently frothy portrait by Watteau into "a picture of decadent bourgeois privilege in the disintegration of feudal society." Or turn to the entry for Cranach the Elder's exquisite Madonna. The painting is as exotic as a tango, all gorgeous reds and oranges, the sensuous drape of velvet and satins, the Madonna's spiraling hair, and the wonderful apples hanging over her head like planets, a crown of glowing planets. In the official text, though, all this is reduced to an "instructive religious artifact from the Teutonic cult of Mary." Marina sometimes will conveniently forget the worst of her script when she is guiding her tours and just let the paintings speak for themselves, but Viktor would never contemplate such a dangerous omission. Having barely survived the purges that decimated the Archaeology Department, along with much of the intelligentsia of Leningrad, he has since grown fluent in the language of the Party.

Even Viktor, though, seems to sense how far short of entertainment his lecture is falling. As he is recounting the laborious process by which language scholars have begun deciphering the various cuneiform inscriptions, he stops midsentence. He runs his finger down the page, murmurs, "Well, perhaps we may dispense with some of this," and skips to the next page. It is only nearing the finish that Viktor leaves the track of his original manuscript and bends to the upcoming occasion. "It may seem," he says, looking past Marina and Nadezhda to address an imaginary gathering, "that the fate of a long-dead culture is far removed from the present concerns of the valiant soldiers gathered here tonight. And yet, if we may conclude anything from the fate of Urartu, it is that feudal systems of oppression are eventually defeated and forgotten. When future archaeologists unearth the forgotten ruins of Fascist Germany"—Viktor pauses to clear his throat, and Marina is startled to see his lower lip quivering with suppressed emotion—"surely," he continues, "surely, comrades, they will be astonished at the vainglorious claims of a Thousand Year Reich."

Nadezhda claps her hands enthusiastically. "It is inspired, Viktor," she says. "They will be on their feet."

"Yes, Uncle. They will certainly be impressed," Marina concurs.

"In fact," Nadezhda adds, "I would be surprised if you are not given a supplemental fee."

"What do you mean?" Viktor's voice is suddenly sharp.

"I mean something beyond the four hundred grams of butter. Out of gratitude."

"Haven't I told you I will bring back what I can? Can you think of nothing but your damned sweets?" Slow starvation has carved the contours of his face into hard bones and made his glare even more stern. "I share my ration with you, even though you are entitled to less, but still you torment me with this incessant ranting."

Nadezhda has been plotting all week what they will make with the butter. Without work to distract her, she talks of nothing else, circling fixedly around her limited options. They have no flour, but she has squirreled away a few pieces of the blockade candy that could be melted down to make shortbread. And if only they had a bit of jam. She has pestered Viktor repeatedly about trading away the vodka.

Now she pouts. "It's easy for you to mock me. You will be feasting tomorrow night while Marina and I eat nothing but bread."

Viktor explodes, not caring that his voice echoes off the frozen walls of the vault and carries through the shelter.

"This is my life's work, Nadezhda. If I die, this is my legacy to the world."

"Yes, it is all that matters to you anymore, this book. You don't even care anymore what has become of your own children."

She is not prepared for the blow, and it knocks her back onto the pallet. She sits down hard but doesn't react. Mutely staring at the wall of carpets, she seems oblivious to the hoarse whispers coming from the other side.

Viktor too is stunned. He mumbles something incomprehensible and then sinks down at the foot of the pallet, his head in his hands.

Marina watches him guardedly from her corner. He is not a violent man, in fact he prides himself on his self-control, but hunger has eaten away the veneer of civilization, and people are not themselves. She has heard terrible things. In the cellars, she hears mothers beat their hungry children when they cry. In the bread lines, young boys rip the bread from the hands of feeble women, and there are rumors of missing children and black market sausage. Liliia Pavlova told her last week about a corpse on the street with its buttocks carved out.

Viktor stands up and trudges to where the candle has been left burning. He blows it out, and Marina hears him cross back to the pallet he and Nadezhda share. He murmurs to his wife, telling her to lift her legs, to get under the blankets. As silently as possible, Marina crawls under her own mountain of blankets and disappears under its comforting, muffling weight.

She wakes up in the night, crying.

"*Izvinite,*" she is whimpering. I'm sorry. When Dmitri reaches over and touches her back, she flinches and jerks away. "I can't help you," she snaps in Russian.

"It's okay," he says. "It's okay, my darling." He pats her back absently, still half-asleep himself. The shoulder of his pajamas is damp with her tears.

"I must go home," she tells him.

"Not tonight."

"No, I must go home. It's urgent. I have to take this chocolate back. They are waiting for me."

"You've had a nightmare, Marinochka. It's okay now." Throughout their married life, not often but once in a while, she has had nightmares. He has them, too, but even in his sleep, he is guarded. Marina wakes him, flailing and muttering things that Dmitri doesn't always understand. Sometimes she cries out, and in the first years of their marriage, there was frequently one name, or he thought it was a name, though not one he recognized. Once, more than fifty years ago, he almost asked, but something stopped him, and now it doesn't matter. It hasn't mattered for a long time.

"I must be home before it's dark," she says. "They are wait-ing and . . ." She stops and shudders. "Where am I?" She sits upright and looks around, frightened.

It is nearly dark in the room, but ambient light from the marina seeps through the curtains and tints the darkness green.

"We're on Drake Island. At the inn. Remember?" he asks, though he knows she will not.

"We're on an island?"

"Where Andrei has his dacha. We were there this evening."

"I must go home." Her voice is as plaintive as a child's.

"We'll go home Monday morning. After the wedding. Go back to sleep now."

But she has swung her legs over the side of the bed and is on her feet, at the window, pulling open the curtain, peer-ing out into the dark. And then she explains again about the chocolate—there isn't enough for him, she is sorry, but she has to take it home.

"I don't want any chocolate."

"Can I go home now?"

"Not tonight."

"They are waiting for me."

"They will be okay."

"Where am I?"

He is so tired. His eyes are leaden, and his mind is swim-ming in deep, heavy water. He answers her questions, but each one costs him an effort. Sometimes it is more than he can bear, this repetition, over and over, of the same questions, the same answers, as though their lives were a battered phonograph record with a hundred skips and they will never get to the end of it.

"Come back to bed," he pleads.

"Where am I?"

When he pulls himself up onto his elbows, he feels the exhaustion in his bones.

"Marina, you have to sleep now." He feels his eyes stinging with frustration. "I need for you to help me. Do you understand?" In the half-light, their eyes meet. What he finds there is her, but also not her. Her eyes are like the bright surface of shallow water, reflecting back his own gaze. Something flutters and darts under the surface, but it might be his own desire, his own memory. He is, he realizes, probably alone.

"Please, Marina. I miss you."

Obediently, she crawls back into their bed and pulls the covers up over her chest. She asks him again, but hesitantly this time, if they can go home, she wants to go home.

"Monday morning, we'll go home. Go to sleep now." His voice is husky. He is holding her and smoothing her hair, her neck. His fingertips know the shape of her back, each little knob of her spine, the soft folds of her waist. If she were lost, he could find her in the dark by touch alone.

She relaxes a little into the crook of his arm. The smell of her, warm and yeasty and faintly scented with lavender, is familiar and potent. She has been in his life for so long that he can hardly recall a time before her. Over the years, they have grown together, their flesh and their thoughts twining so closely that he cannot imagine the person he might be apart from her.

Even during the war, when they were physically separated, she was there with him in the form of a small studio photograph taken to mark her graduation. When his unit was encircled at Chudovo and he was captured by the Germans, he held on to the photograph and began whispering to it like an icon. For three years, he worked in the German prison camps, first in the Ukraine and later in Bavaria, where starving prisoners logged the forest and cut railroad ties. He kept the photograph in his breast pocket and, while working, he would dredge up and replay every conversation with her that he could remember. Later, he invented new ones, talking with her under his breath. The Germans thought he had gone crazy. She listened as he confessed his cowardice, his fear of the sadistic guards, and his humiliating physical needs. At night, her delicate hands came to him in sleep, stroking his face, his chest, his penis.

He survived the war, but when the American soldiers came to liberate the camp, he was already a dead man. Being captured by the Germans was treason: Stalin had said as much. Dmitri knew what that meant—he had lost his father in prison—he could never go home again. Dazed and without hope, he slipped out of the camp and joined the millions of refugees wandering the roads through the rubble of Germany. He stayed safely inside the American occupation zone and for nearly three months managed to avoid the dragnets rounding up Soviets for forced repatriation. But he had no papers, no money, and eventually he was caught filching eggs from a hen-house, beaten severely by the enraged farmer, and rescued just this side of death by American soldiers. A week later, he was behind barbed wire again, this time in a refugee camp. He had heard rumors of others who had committed suicide rather than return to the Soviet Union, and he noted that the soldiers took his belt.

On his third day in the camp, walking down the main corridor between the barracks, he saw a woman up ahead who looked like Marina. He was not surprised; he had lost his glasses when he was captured, and from a distance, many women appeared to be Marina. But as he drew closer, she did not resolve into a stranger, and when she turned and saw him staring at her, she cried out his name.

Fifty-eight years later, this single moment still astonishes him. It is the one event in his long life that is both wildly illogical and absolutely necessary. Everything else he can consign to the random happenstance of a godless world, but not this moment.

He remembers they stood stock-still before each other, stunned into speechlessness. Tentatively, he reached out and ran his fingers over her face like a blind man, rubbing a tear from her cheek, astonished at its materiality. And then he looked down and saw that she was not alone. There was a child, a solemn toddler that watched him unblinkingly from behind her legs.

"This is our son," she said, drawing the boy forward. "I named him Andrei," and nothing more.

What were the odds that a single act of lovemaking might result in a child? Another man might have doubted her, might have questioned whether she had met someone after he left for the front. Or worse. He had witnessed the depravities, the vodka-fueled rapes of old women and children, and the desperate licentiousness of starving women. Later, she told him how she and her infant had evacuated from Leningrad and survived the journey to a small resort town in the Caucasus only to arrive a few short weeks before the Wehrmacht overran and occupied it. She had scratched out an existence doing laundry for the officers there, and a year later, with the Red Army threatening to retake the town, had retreated with those officers all the way back to Munich, where she spent the remainder of the war in a munitions factory. Another man might have wondered if this child was German.

But he had just been handed back his life. It was a miracle—it embarrasses him to think in such terms, but there is no other word for it—and he would not spit on it. Instead, he threw himself into saving what had been given him, forging new identities as Polish Ukrainians for himself and Marina and the boy so that they could emigrate to America. They made a new life, learned a new language, found work, made a home. They even had a second child, a leap of faith in their future. And both of them did their best not to look back, lest they turn into pillars of salt. If they spoke at all of the war, they were as careful as the official censors back in the Soviet Union to mention only the victories and the acts of heroism.

It didn't matter. The bond that had first brought them together as children existed whether they spoke of it or not, the bond of survivors. Here in America, a relentlessly foolish and optimistic country, what they knew drew them closer together. She was his country and he hers. They were inseparable.

Until now. She is leaving him, not all at once, which would be painful enough, but in a wrenching succession of separations. One moment she is here, and then she is gone again, and each journey takes her a little farther from his reach. He cannot follow her, and he wonders where she goes when she leaves.

Listen. Coming up the Main Staircase, you can hear them, their raucous laughter and shouted toasts. "The king drinks!" they cry. There is a party in progress in the Snyders Room, a feast to celebrate the Day of the Three Kings. The traditional pie has been baked, and the older man in the middle there must have gotten the piece with the bean inside, because he is wearing the crown of the Bean King. He is surrounded by a tight composition of happy, jostling couples, children, and even a babe in arms. "The king drinks!" Glasses are raised. Do you see that fellow standing behind him with the upraised pitcher? That is the Bean King's son-in-law, the painter himself. And there is Jordaens's wife, Yelizabeth. Oh, and over here, look at this, this fellow in the jester's cap, with one hand reaching out for Jordaens's pitcher while the other slips casually down the front of this woman's bodice. "The king drinks! The king drinks!" There they go again. They are boisterous, rollicking. The only stillness in the painting is in the lower right corner, a hound whose eyes are focused with canine intensity on the ham in the Bean King's lap.

Her granddaughter is getting married. Katie, the girl with the braces. And the groom, whose name escapes her just now.

The lawn is thronged with wedding guests. They mingle and shake hands and hug each other. A string quartet is posted down by the beach on a half circle of folding chairs, and strains of Bach waft up on the early-afternoon breezes.

Marina stands just inside the gate, hesitating. She has difficulty with large groups of people; there are so many faces to keep straight, so many sensations to organize. It is almost dizzying, the blur of faces, the rustle of stiff fabrics, the perfume of so many bodies.

Standing at the gate, she appears to be a greeter, so people make a point to stop and shake her hand. She smiles and says that it's a lovely day. "It's so good to see you," she adds when she suspects that this person may be someone she should know.

Finally, the guests have all arrived and assembled near the beach.

"Papa, we're going to get started pretty soon." It is their son, Andrei. He is dressed in a dark suit and looks uncommonly handsome.

"Good morning, beautiful." He kisses Marina on each cheek and then offers her his arm. "Are you ready to sit down?"

"Will you sit next to me?" she asks coyly.

"I can't. I have to give Katie away. But Papa will sit with you, okay?" Marina nods. Andrei walks them to their seats where Helen is waiting for them. She slides her purse off the seat next to her.

"Did you say hello to everyone, Mama?"

"I think so."

"Who's the woman in the hat?"

"Who?"

"Over there."

Marina looks in the direction Helen is nodding. There is a woman in a big blue hat like a flying saucer, but it's not someone she recognizes. She shakes her head. "I don't know."

"You were talking to her for a long time."

"Oh, well, she was very nice. I think this is her home."

"You should see Katie. I went upstairs a little while ago. She looks so beautiful."

"You look beautiful, too," Marina tells her daughter.

Helen shrugs off the compliment, but then impulsively takes her mother's hand and squeezes it. "I . . ." she starts to say something, but then just gives her mother's hand another squeeze.

The music is triumphal, and the guests rise and turn to view the approaching bride. She is indeed beautiful, luminous and happy. Andrei is stricken but resolutely delivers her to the handsome young man who has robbed him of his own youth. The company of attendants arrayed on either side of the bride and groom are sober with the unanticipated import of this moment. And looking around, one can see on the faces of the assembled family and guests the best of their humanity radiating a collective warmth around this fledgling young couple. There is music and tears and words. *Commitment* and *love* and *cherish* and *community* and *honor*.

And music and more words. Olga Markhaeva recites poetry, and Anya sings a song she remembers from her childhood, romantic and sweet. If Marina lives to be eighty, she thinks, she will never forget this wonderful night.

Such a feast! There is the butter, but also American cheese and boiled pearl barley in silky fat and a bottle of vodka. They have invited guests to share the spoils Viktor has brought back from the front. Sergei Pavlovich and his sister Liliia have contributed a handful of dried apricots that Nadezhda boiled down to make a glaze for her shortbread. Anya has brought an onion, which they slice into wafers.

Paper lanterns are strung from the pipes and a white linen tablecloth laid over the bare wooden table. On the table is arranged an extravagant array of delicacies. They light not one but three candles, and the dank little room in the cellar flickers with light, still cold but bright with the illusion of warmth. Even the sound of shells exploding in the world above them can't dampen their high spirits. With thimblefuls of vodka, they toast the Red Army's advances toward Tikhvin, they toast the brave sons and daughters of the Soviet Union, they toast the great fortune of food and friends with whom to share it. It is enough to make them feel drunk, the vodka and the sharp bite of onion and the melting sweetness of shortbread. They ravish the food like lovers. Afterward, they listen as Olga recites Anna Akhmatova's poems. Her voice, by day clipped and hard, is slow as a deep river, and the candlelight transforms her profile, softening the broad planes of her forehead and nose, and sparkling in her damp eyes.

Somewhere there is a simple life and a world,
Transparent, warm, joyful . . .
There at evening a neighbor talks with a girl
Across the fence, and only the bees can hear
This most tender murmuring of all.

But we live ceremoniously and with difficulty
And we observe the rites of our bitter meetings,
When suddenly the reckless wind
Breaks off a sentence just begun—

But not for anything would we exchange this splendid
Granite city of fame and calamity,
The wide rivers of glistening ice,
The sunless, gloomy gardens,
And barely audible, the muse's voice.

Sated, Nadezhda nestles into Viktor's arm like a schoolgirl and he kisses the top of her head. Marina sees Liliia and Sergei mopping their eyes. It feels luxuriant, these warm tears on a full stomach. They are happy.

Later that night, they will retch into slop pails at the foot of their cots. Their bodies have forgotten how to digest such richness. Still, they won't feel hungry for days.

The Majolica Room. So called because it holds the museum's collection of the Italian style of decorative pottery. By happy accident, the room itself evokes majolica, being brightly painted in yellows and greens with Renaissance motifs.

Most famously, the room contains the museum's two Raphaels, the Conestabile Madonna and the *Holy Family*. There is an apocryphal story that this room once held a third Raphael, another Madonna and child. According to an elderly room attendant, it was, like the Conestabile, a tondo, or round painting, "about the size of a beach ball" and in an elaborate gilt frame. If the woman is to be believed (and really, her story cannot be vouched for) the Madonna in this painting is seated in a field, with the Christ Child standing on her lap. At her side is another slightly older child dressed in animal skins and no doubt representing a young John the Baptist. This older child is handing a small cross to the Christ Child, who accepts it, and all three figures are gazing on the cross as though they can see into the future. She provides other details, that the Madonna is dressed in Roman garb and holds a small gilt-edged book in her hand, a prayer book perhaps, that the background is a delicately colored landscape and in the foreground are white flowers.

No painting in the museum's holdings answers to this description. Though the details she has provided are consistent with Raphael's style, there is absolutely no corroborating evidence to support her claim, and it is likely that she has merely confused it with the Conestabile Madonna.

The radio fell silent at the beginning of the month and the last newspaper went to print on December 12. Even the bombing has stopped. There is nothing left now to distract them from the miseries of cold and hunger except their own internal resources. And so, as the world gets smaller and colder and dimmer, Marina notices, people are becoming fixated. Most fixate on their physical miseries, spending hours running their tongues over swollen gums or opening and shutting the same cupboard in search of food that is not there. But others disown their shriveling bodies and fixate instead on an idea.

Uncle Viktor has become increasingly obsessed with finishing his history of Urartu. He worries that he may die before he completes it, and that this unearthed history will die with him. Marina lies in bed late into the night and listens to the feverish scratching of his pen. It has gotten so cold in the cellars that ink freezes, and so he must constantly stop and warm the bottle in his hands. But then a few minutes later, the scratching will start again. Sometimes he writes late into the night until he collapses at his desk.

In another corner of Bomb Shelter #3, the architect Alexander Nikolsky also has his fixation. He sketches so incessantly that at the end of the day his fist will not unclench to release his pencil. The other night, he staged a showing of these drawings. He lined up chairs in his corner of the cellar, leaned one drawing against the back of each chair, and invited his neighbors to come view his work.

And when they came, what people saw was not art such as they had expected but drawings of the actual room where they stood. He had sketched interiors of the cellar and its residents, odd little drawings of their makeshift lodgings. Sketch after sketch showed the low vaulted ceilings crossed with pipes, the clutter of furniture, and the stark shadows cast by a single oil lamp. He had also sketched the rooms upstairs, some drawings all but black, others portraying eerily gothic scenes with figures dwarfed in huge, vacant spaces. One drawing showed merely a hand with three marble-size pieces of bread resting in the palm.

What struck Marina was the roughness of the drawings, their looming shapes and smudgy darkness. That and the human figures, faceless and interchangeable. She didn't know if this was his intention, but they had the quality of nightmares.

Nikolsky pondered this. "My intention was not to suggest anything but what is. These are not meant to be art. They are documentation, so that those who come later will know how we lived," he said.

Marina was reminded uncomfortably of her uncle recording the history of the lost civilization of Urartu.

"But surely," Marina said to Nikolsky, "some here will live to tell the story themselves."

"Oh, yes," Nikolsky agreed pleasantly. "But who will believe them?"

Marina has her memory palace: that has become her fixation.

She can now walk anywhere in the picture gallery, and the sculptures and paintings appear so readily in her mind that she can rattle most of them off without thinking. What started as an exercise, a distraction, has come to seem like the very point of her existence. But if she had to justify that point, she would be at a loss. There are no books, no drawings, nothing to show for nearly three months of practice.

"That is the point," Anya says. "Your uncle and Alexander Nikolsky are wise men, I'm sure, but they trust too much to paper. No one can take away what is in here." She taps her forehead.

"Yes, no one can take it away, but no one else can see it, either, Anya."

"Don't give up just yet, dear."

Marina sighs.

One day shortly after they began their little tours, Anya stopped in the Titian Room, pointed to a place on the wall, and then, in a conspiratorial whisper, described a painting that Marina had never seen.

Anya breathed into Marina's ear. "They took it away."

"Why do you whisper, Auntie?" Marina asked. "It's not a secret that paintings went to Moscow. Everyone knows this." About ten years ago, Stalin forced the Hermitage to send a large part of its holdings, including some four hundred old masters, to the Museum of Fine Arts in exchange for some Impressionists and Post-Impressionists which were too decadent to display. The professors at the academy used to talk quite openly about it, though of course they were careful to couch the rape of the museum in the most veiled of euphemisms.

Anya shook her head and whispered, "Not the paintings that

went to Moscow. Others. Before that. Before you were born." She glanced around again, as though someone might be hiding in the empty room. "They would come and the next morning things would be missing," Anya said, raising her eyebrows knowingly.

"Who?"

"I never saw them, but it was well known that they were from the Antiquariat."

According to Anya, all through the twenties, Stalin's agents came to Orbeli with lists and left in the night with art to be sold on the international market. When the room attendants and museum guides came to work in the morning, they would find that art was missing and that the remaining paintings had been rehung in the night to disguise the gaps. Curators and directors made no mention of the vanished work and rebuffed any questions, and quickly it was understood that, officially, this art had never existed. Anya says that, years before the official deacquisitions, hundreds of other pieces disappeared one by one: paintings and sculpture and enough silver to fill a pirate ship.

But Anya can recall these paintings as easily as those that are still part of the collection, and she has come up with a scheme to include all these missing works in Marina's memory palace. Never mind that Marina has never seen them herself. This has become Anya's fixation.

"If no one is left to remember them," Anya said when she first hatched this lunatic notion, "then it is as though they never existed."

Marina agreed that this was sad but protested the logic of trying to remember something she had never seen. But Anya was not interested in reason. "I could die any day now," she answered, "and when I do, they should not die with me."

It is impossible to argue, as she shows every sign of being near death. The many layers of clothing everyone must pile on against the cold conceal the worst ravages of starvation, but Anya is increasingly frail, hardly able to bear even the weight of her own bones. Walking tires her, and she can take only a few steps without having to rest. Her health alone would seem to be reason enough to abandon walking the palace and burning precious calories unnecessarily, but Anya is adamant, and Marina suspects that this need to pass on what she remembers is the only thing keeping her alive.

So now Marina is trying to relearn the rooms, adding another layer of vanished paintings over the ones she already knows. Anya describes the missing canvas in detail, and while Marina can't actually visualize it, she commits enough to memory to appease her friend. It is tedious work, and even though they get up earlier and earlier, their progress has slowed to a crawl. They have not yet made it past the New Hermitage rooms or across the courtyard to the rooms in the Winter Palace, and some days they cannot even get up the stairs.

This morning, though, Anya is determined to visit the Rembrandt Room, where she says she has much to show Marina.

The Main Staircase inside the New Hermitage is treacherous with ice, and there are no handrails to prevent a fall. Anya leans heavily on Marina, and the two edge up one step at a time, like mountain climbers on a treacherous slope. It takes them half an hour to reach the top. They traverse the long landing, passing empty marble pedestals, and come to the first room beyond the staircase, where the van Dykes hung. Anya pulls a rag from the pocket of her jacket. She is loath to admit how exhausted she is, so while she rests she makes a show of inspecting

131

a large frame leaning against the wall. She carefully wipes away dust that has settled along the top edge.

Marina stands at her side and looks around the vacant room. In some ways, it is more beautiful now. Stripped of the paintings and furnishings, the room itself comes to the fore, austere and grand. Frost has etched elaborate patterns across the walls, swirls that glitter in the morning light. Still, the empty frames remind one of all the people who are missing. The Earl of Danby and Queen Henrietta. Charles the First in his armor and Thomas Wharton with his feathered hat. A new family with a baby girl and a pair of young sisters dressed in their finery. The elder sister gazes proudly at Marina as she passes and identifies them, Elizabeth and Philadelphia Wharton, but the younger one looks as though she would like to be released from the uncomfortable pose that the artist has put her in.

There are others that she cannot see, but last week Anya described every detail of the paintings, and so when Marina passes the approximate spots where they hung, she calls back to Anya, still lingering near the door, describing a lord and then a lady and, last, a mother and daughter.

"She's wearing a crimson dress and a ruff," Marina says. "And the daughter, who is about seven or eight, stands to her left. She looks like a little adult in her dress."

"Can you picture them?" Anya asks hopefully.

"Maybe a little," Marina lies.

She circles nearly back to where Anya is still standing. Here is the artist van Dyke himself, a romantic-looking man with curls and a long nose. And just beyond him, in the enormous frame that Anya was dusting, is a Madonna and child. They look out of place among all these Flemish gentlefolk. The painting is called *The Rest on the Flight into Egypt,* but two birds on the wing over Mary's head give the painting its nickname, Madonna with Partridges.

"Are you all right now?" she asks Anya.

"Quite," Anya says.

Marina takes her arm. "If we want to get to the Rembrandts today, I think we'd better keep moving." And so the two of them walk, arm in arm, through the Rubens Room. They are moving so slowly that Marina can give a running commentary, though she skips over a few pieces. She resolutely ignores Bacchus and wills his corpulence to fade back to silvery frost, merely noting for the record that he is there. The same goes for Rubens's painting of the daughter suckling her starving father.

"*Mars and Cupid. Venus and Adonis. The Coronation of the Virgin. Hagar Leaving the House of Abraham.*"

At this pace, even if they turn around now, she will be late for work. She assists the museum carpenter in the construction of coffins. The museum's storerooms are the only remaining source of lumber in the city, and so coffin building has become the main occupation of the displaced workers on the staff. They are not craftsmen, but then again these are the most utilitarian of boxes, a few boards of pine slapped together to hold bodies that weigh next to nothing. There are so many workers out ill now that those who are still able are driven even harder trying to keep up with the demand. If she is late, she had better have a very good reason. Something better than strolling the picture gallery and cataloging missing art.

When they get to the Tent Hall, Marina moves them right down the center of the hall, not even bothering to comment on what is on either side of her. She expects Anya to scold her, but the old woman has also focused her attention on the doorway at the end of the hall leading to the Rembrandt Room. Halfway down the length of the hall, Anya suddenly weaves and then grabs at Marina's chest.

"I'm fine," she says, still gripping Marina's jacket. "I just lost my balance there."

"We really should turn around, Anya. You're looking tired. Besides, I'll need to go to work soon."

Anya pulls herself upright and releases Marina. "If you must go, you must go. I will go on to the Rembrandt Room." She picks up the pace, weaving wildly toward the doorway, as if to suggest that it is Marina who is holding them up.

"Okay, okay, slow down," Marina says, taking her arm again and steadying her. "We don't need to get there yesterday."

Just inside the door, Anya stops in front of the wall that held *Danae,* but her eyes move beyond the right edge of the frame. "This was one of the first," she says. "I came to work one morning and he was gone. Quite full of himself, don't you think?"

It is all Marina can do not to remind Anya that she has never seen this painting, whatever it is. "Who is he?" she asks.

"Oh, well, Rembrandt said he was a Polish nobleman, but he doesn't look like any Pole I've ever seen. He's Russian. Look." She points. "He's got that bearskin cap and the fur cloak like they used to wear here. And that big pearl earring. He thinks he's quite the catch with that mustache of his, but look at those jowls under his chin."

"And what was it called?"

Anya pulls out of her reverie and gives Marina a sharp look, as though she has asked a foolish question. "*A Polish Nobleman.*"

A Polish Nobleman, pearl earring, mustache, bearskin cap. Okay, good enough.

"Now that one looks a bit like you," Anya says, pointing to the next wall. "But younger. She's got your red hair, though."

Anya goes on to describe a girl leaning on a broom and looking directly at the viewer. *Girl with a Broom.* And then a portrait of a lady with a carnation, and another one of Pallas Athene, and another of an old man.

"Now here is the scene where Peter denied Christ. This was one of his best, in my opinion."

"Another one?" Marina wonders if perhaps Anya is confused. It's hard to believe that Stalin would sell off so many masterpieces. Hasn't he always said that this art belongs to the people, that it is their heritage? She is not so naive as to believe everything she is told, but to sell even one Rembrandt seems inconceivable. Anya has already described half a dozen.

"Do you know this story, Marina? At the last supper, Christ told Peter that he would deny knowing him. Before the cock crowed three times. And the Gospels tell us that this is in fact what happened. You see him here"—she points—"he is sitting around the fire with some people in the town. Romans. Now, this is the touch of the master. Rembrandt used the firelight to make the scene more dramatic."

Anya's voice blurs behind the thought taking shape in Marina's mind. She knows Anya wouldn't lie outright, but might these all be fabrications? Might Anya have invented these paintings? They are very specific visions, but that doesn't mean they are real.

"Are you sure it was a Rembrandt?"

Anya turns very slowly to Marina. "When you see it, you'll

know." Her eyes are as bright and blank as coins. "No one else could paint like that."

Marina determines in that moment to ask Olga Markhaeva if she's ever heard of these missing paintings. She doesn't know why this didn't occur to her before. Anya is, after all, a very old woman.

The return trip to the stairs is even more protracted, though they are stopping only for Anya to rest. But if Marina is tempted to rush her, one look at Anya dispels the idea. With each step, Anya's appearance grows grayer, and soon Marina is half carrying her, Anya's feet dragging almost weightlessly.

They stop again near the Madonna with Partridges. She slumps Anya against a marble vase, propping her up with one hand. Anya is perilously close to collapsing to the floor, and if she does, Marina isn't at all sure she will be able to get her up again.

The Madonna is also resting. Holding her baby in her lap, she looks distracted and even a bit alarmed by a flock of putti who are dancing ring-around-the-rosy nearby. She doesn't look at all anxious to take on anyone else's troubles. But Marina petitions her anyway. She's not asking for much. "Help me get her downstairs," she whispers. "Don't let her die here, please." She adds another "please" for good measure and with her free hand furtively touches her fingers to her forehead.

The Rubens Room. Even here, in a room riotous with flesh, the painting at the center of the long wall gives one pause. Here is a young woman suckling an old man. She is young and plump and fresh-faced. He is naked, with only a black cloth draped over his genitals. His hands are bound in chains behind his back. Although his musculature is beautiful—the arms and legs fully sculpted, the chest and abdomen defined—his head is a horror: the beard and hair matted, the eyes bulging as grotesquely as a gargoyle's and focused downward on the girl's exposed nipple.

Before you either turn away in disgust or wink knowingly at one another, you should know that the artist insists that this is a picture about love. Filial love. The old man has been condemned by the Roman senate to die of hunger, and his daughter has come to his prison cell and offered her breast to feed him. This has nothing to do with the decorous love or amorous passions one is more accustomed to seeing in a painting. It is raw and wretched and demeaning. In the end, we are physical bodies and every abstract notion about love sinks beneath this fact.

"Doesn't she look beautiful, Mama? The something old is Naureen's pearls."

"She reminds me of a girl I knew once."

"Who was that?"

"Back in Leningrad. I don't know—I forget her name now. She was upstairs."

"Was this when you lived in the cellar?"

"Yes. I would go upstairs and visit her."

"I don't understand something. Why were you living in a cellar?"

"It was the war. They were dropping bombs."

"Oh. Of course. That makes sense."

"We all lived in the cellars then."

"But not your friend who lived upstairs?"

"No."

"Why not her?"

"I don't know. I can't remember."

"It's okay, you don't have to. I was just curious."

"Her father died of starvation that winter. I remember that. She fed him with her breast milk, but he died anyway."

Sleds have appeared on Nevsky Prospekt, throughout the city, children's sleds painted red and yellow and blue. The tramcars have long since stopped running, frozen wherever they happened to be on their runs when the last of the electricity shut down. To get from one place to another, people walk. The streets are nearly deserted, but a few people trudge in slow motion, their bodies bent forward as if into a stiff wind. Some pull sleds, ferrying those who can no longer walk. The lame. The dead. Corpses wrapped in swaddling or still bundled in their heavy coats. Blue feet protrude. The only sounds on the street are the terrible squeaking of runners on ice.

Marina struggles over a hummock of frozen snow on the sidewalk. She has been walking for more than two hours and has journeyed five blocks from the service entrance of the New Hermitage, a distance she once traveled in an abstracted heartbeat, giving it no more of her attention than she gave to breathing. Now it is like being in a dream and trying to run from something: her legs will not move, they are inanimate wood, rooted into the ground, and only with a concentrated effort of will can she heave one stump off the ground, push it forward, then set it down again gingerly, feeling for the slide of ice beneath her boot before she shifts her weight.

She rests, breathless and dizzy from the exertion, and reaches out her hand to rest it against the stone front of a building for support. Slowly, she lifts her eyes up from the ground. The flat gray sky reels momentarily before stabilizing.

She is only a few blocks from the Krasnov apartment, but though this is her neighborhood, she hardly recognizes it. Hoarfrost covers every surface, and icicles hang like moss from the wires and eaves above her. The buildings, too, are crusted over with ice, and their boarded windows present a blank face to the street. There is no noise, no dogs or cats in the street, no smoke drifting up from the chimneys, no evidence at all of life. She might be the sole remaining survivor of a lost civilization, like Uncle Viktor's Urartu. The doomed citizenry has left behind messages, however, plastered on the plywood and walls and sealed under ice, but still legible. Here is a poster with the uplifting pronouncement "Victory Is Near." Another official poster commands the reader to seek shelter during air raids and threatens severe penalties for failing to do so. Beneath these, at eye level, is a frozen collage of typed and handwritten notices: offers to exchange shoes, a mahogany armoire, a bicycle, gold and silver jewelry, a morocco-bound set of travel journals, a sable coat, a typewriter. Whatever one might want is advertised here, all in exchange for foodstuffs. They are old, the ragged scraps of paper smeared and buried under layers of frost. The last desperate pleas of the civilization, they were posted here back when one might still conceivably barter for food. There are no fresh notices.

In this new geography, the next corner recedes into the distant horizon like the forced perspective in landscapes, hazy gray and impossibly far away, separated by a rolling mountain range of compacted dirty snow and studded with frozen hills of trash and slick lakes of ice. She resolutely turns her attention back to her legs, to the next step. In front of her, she holds out the image of a chocolate bar.

Today is Tatiana's birthday, and Nadezhda was particularly distressed this morning on account of the day. She cannot admit the too-crushing possibility that her children are dead, so she focused her grief instead on the idea of her little girl celebrating her birthday without family around her. She reminisced distract-edly about past birthday celebrations, the cakes that she used to bake for her children, cakes filled with jam and frosted with buttercream, the cocoa, the wrapped gifts heaped on the birth-day child's plate. She remembered hiding a toy rifle, a packet of crayons, and a bar of chocolate for Mikhail's last birthday, tucking them under some linens on a high shelf where the boy wouldn't think to look. In the distracted tumult of the children's leaving, she had forgotten about them until that moment.

"I expected him to be back before his birthday." She turned on her husband with a sudden fury. "You promised me they would come home in two weeks."

Viktor looked up at her, his dull eyes filled with pain, but he didn't say anything. He hasn't gotten out of bed for ten days now, and in that time his appearance has undergone a disquiet-ing transformation. His face is a skeletal mask, his nose grown sharp, his eyes hollow.

Marina cut off her aunt before she could further berate her sick husband. "Are they still there?"

"Where?" Nadezhda asked, confused.

"The gifts. The chocolate. Is it still there?"

Nadezhda was too distraught to understand the significance of the question, but Marina was already planning this journey. Chocolate, probably a large bar, given Nadezhda's tendency to indulge her children. Even now, Marina can taste the velvety sweetness in her mouth.

When she turns off Nevsky and onto her street, she is wrenched by the view of Number Nineteen, her home. The face of the building has been peeled away by an explosive, exposing the front apartments to the street like the rooms of a dollhouse. The ground floor is buried in rubble but she can see right into the rooms on the first floor. In one room, a yellow kitchen, chairs are strewn on the floor but an unbroken teacup sits on the table. A calendar hangs askew over the stove. This would be the Magrachev family's apartment, Marina thinks, a factory supervisor and his wife, her elderly father, and a little girl Mikhail's age. In the adjoining room, a light fixture still hangs from the ceiling, its shade rocking in a gust of wind. Two coats, a man's and a woman's, hang on pegs near the door.

The front entrance to the building, once beautiful Italian marble with two etched-glass doors, is demolished, so Marina makes her slow way around to the side yard. Rubble and refuse is heaped in the yard in frozen piles. She rings the bell and waits. She rings again. Perhaps everyone has left. It doesn't seem possible that anyone could still be living here, and she is on the verge of tears. She has no door key for the service entrance. All this way for nothing. She cannot feel her legs, and it is impossible to believe that they will carry her back over the distance she has come.

And then the door opens a crack.

"Who is it?" A hoarse voice crackles, and the face of an ancient hag peers around the doorjamb.

"It's Marina from Five East."

"Marina Anatolyevna Krasnova?"

Marina realizes with a start that the hag is Vera Yurievna, the building's janitor, a woman in her early forties. The door opens wide and Vera throws her arms around Marina and hugs her as though Marina were a long-lost relation.

"You're a block of ice, child. Come in, come in. I'll put some water on the stove," she offers, and draws Marina inside and down a black hallway to her apartment.

Vera lights a candle that gutters, spitting flickers of light into the gloom and revealing a dank little warren. She has moved into her kitchen, boarding up the window and closing off the other room. Into this room she has moved a narrow bed, a single chair, and a small table, all arranged around a *burzhuika,* the ubiquitous little iron stove that everyone uses now.

She offers Marina the chair and pulls a blanket off the rumpled heaps on the bed. "Here, put this around you. We'll have some heat in a moment." The blanket is still warm from Vera's body, and Marina accepts it gratefully.

Vera starts a fire, all the while asking after Marina's family, her aunt, her uncle, the two little chicks. She pulls a book off the table, a collection of fables, and tears out two pages, crumples them, and places them in the stove. This is followed by what is clearly part of a table leg. Vera lights the paper and carefully nurses the flame into a tidy little fire.

"Pull that chair closer. Warm your hands." Then she dribbles some water from a jug into the kettle and sets it back on the stove.

"Are you the only one here?" Marina asks. As much as she hates being cheek by jowl with the crowds huddled in the basements of the Hermitage, this desolation seems a far worse alternative.

"Oh, no. Of course, a lot of them left after the shelling, moved in with friends or whomever."

"When was that?"

"December twelfth, just after midnight. Terrible." Vera stares into some private vision. "Terrible."

"But there are still twenty-three of us. The apartments in the rear are unharmed. Your apartment is just as you left it. Anna Ostromovna Dudin and her mother, next door to you, they're still here. And there's seven in Four East, Maria Volkova and her little chicks and three cousins." Vera ticks off the residents still living in the building and the fates of those who have gone. "Sofia Grechina, do you remember her, the poet, that odd woman on the first floor with the two poodles? Her apartment was buried, but she was working the swing shift. You've never seen such hysteria. The two dogs, she had managed to keep them alive, I think she fed them part of her own rations, but of course they were buried in the rubble. She's moved in with Georgi Karasev's mother."

Marina recalls the two coats left hanging on their pegs, the swinging light shade, and asks about the Magrachevs. Vera shakes her head.

The water comes to a boil, and Vera pours it into two porcelain cups.

"To our loved ones at the front," Vera intones and lifts her cup.

Marina cups the warm china in her hands, breathing in the steam and then taking shallow sips. The water is luxuriously hot and cuts a molten swath down Marina's throat to her middle. It feels like new life.

"Oh, goodness, that reminds me," Vera says. "I have a letter for you." She crosses to a shelf and, after a bit of rummaging, produces a thin envelope. "It came a few weeks ago," Vera apologizes. "I was going to forward it to you, but the postwoman has stopped coming."

Her name and address are written out in Dmitri's careful script. The letter trembles in Marina's hands. He is alive. She tears open the envelope and pulls out two sheets. They are ribbed with strips of blue paper pasted over Dmitri's script by the censors.

My dearest Marinochka,

I think of you every moment and hold the image of you in my heart to remind me of why I am here. We are ███████
██

But despite all this, I remain hopeful to see you again soon. Everything reminds me of you. Last night, a girl came to our camp with a goodwill delegation from ████ ████████████. She had your hair and from a distance, she looked so much like you that I called out your name and ran like an idiot halfway across the camp. But, as you know, my distance vision is poor and when I got closer, she actually bore little resemblance to you. I tried to explain my mistake, but I fumbled so, and I think I may have frightened her a little. As a token of apology, I gave her some sunflower seeds.

████████████████████████ but then I feel the warmth

of the sun on my back, and the vivid green of the trees just beyond our camp and I feel hopeful again that ███████████

Marina stops reading, puzzled, and then looks in the upper left corner and finds a date: 21 September 1941. The letter is almost three months old. She feels a flash of anger toward Vera, but before it can bloom she thinks to check the postmark. It reads 28 November.

News comes to us here from the city that ███████████ ███████████████████████ How are your aunt and uncle? And what does he think of our engagement? It occurred to me after I left that perhaps I should have asked him for your hand, and I hope you will tell him that I regret not thinking of this sooner. Perhaps he will not mind so much.

Write to me, dearest, and tell me everything you can think of. It needn't be important, but just the daily things, what you ate for dinner or how the packing is coming. When everything seems so weighted with significance, it is nice to hear of inconsequential things.

Give Tatiana a big hug for me. I don't imagine that Mikhail will endure a hug, but tell him that he must study hard, that he is the hope of our ███████████ country. And for yourself, you must imagine that I am kissing your hair, your eyelids, the tip of your nose, your lips, et cetera. With all my love,
Dima

Vera is watching her face. "Is he well?"
"I don't know. The letter is very old."

146

"I'm sorry, dear. I didn't see that it was yours before the postwoman had gone, or it would have been forwarded."

"No, no. You're not to blame. Thank you for saving it for me." She feels grief welling up inside her, surging like nausea, but she tamps down her thoughts and forces the darkness back down her throat. She carefully refolds the letter, returns it to its envelope, and puts it into her coat pocket.

"I suppose I should go upstairs." She does not tell Vera why she has come, but makes up something about needing to fetch some papers for Uncle Viktor. She has brought her door key but stupidly forgotten to bring a candle, so Vera gives her the stub of her own candle. Her generosity makes Marina ashamed of her secret about the chocolate.

"I hope you don't mind if I don't go up with you," Vera says. "The stairs, you know."

It is a herculean effort to climb up the dizzying stairwell. Marina pulls herself one step at a time up five flights of stairs. By the time she reaches the door to her apartment and turns the key in the lock, she is panting shallowly and can barely find the strength to push open the heavy door.

The dim candlelight laps at a dead gray interior webbed with frost. Uncle Viktor sold off the Oriental carpet in the front room back in October and pieces of the wooden furniture were sold later for firewood, so the room is nearly bare. A lone divan hunkers like a gray beast in the corner.

Marina follows the candlelight into the hall where the linen cupboard is. She doesn't want to look in the other rooms, but when she sees that she will need something to stand on in order to reach the high shelf, she makes a tour of the apartment until she finds a metal footlocker in Viktor and Nadezhda's room.

Even empty, it is too heavy to lift, and as Marina drags it slowly back to the closet, it scrapes a trail across Nadezhda's parquet floors. Finally, she is able to reach the shelf, and she pulls down on top of her head a pile of tablecloths, napkins, doilies, a toy gun. Her hand finds something rectangular, the size of an envelope but heavy in her hand.

She might have eaten it right there, sitting on the metal footlocker, staring down at this miracle in her hand. No one would know. No one. Something desperate works at her gut, and her brain churns, her fingers tremble. What she thinks is that she is holding the life of her uncle in her hands.

It is a terrible thing to have loved ones, people to whom you are shackled by whatever bonds make their pain yours. Although she has no tender feelings for her uncle, her obligation is as strong as love. She recognizes the compact. It is that same sense of duty that has governed his behavior toward her all her life, taking her in and providing for her in spite of his fears. Giving her the larger pieces of bread at every meal, even as he wastes away. Perhaps this is love.

She knows that if she unwraps the foil and exposes the chocolate, the last bit of her that is human will die, and so before she can think any further she stuffs it into her coat pocket with Dmitri's letter. On the way back to the museum, she feels the weight of the chocolate and the letter in her pocket. They bang insistently against her thigh at each step.

It begins to snow, a few flakes at first, but before long the sky is heavy and swirling. The few other stragglers on the boulevard disappear behind a curtain of whiteness, and she moves on alone through the soft blur as though in a nightmare. Her feet are leaden, and though she keeps lifting each foot and setting it down again, she has no sense of moving forward. The landmarks that marked her journey here have disappeared into whiteness, and the snow muffles any sounds. She cannot recall crossing the Griboedova Canal, though surely she must have.

Five, twelve, forty steps. She begins to count in order to reassure herself that she is moving. She must not panic, she must stay calm and keep walking, trusting that each step forward brings her closer to safety. But she is unsure even of this. For all she knows, she may have turned off Nevsky, she may be wandering in the wrong direction. She has no idea where she is, and the whiteness is starting to dim. Soon it will be completely dark, and what will become of her then?

She is up to one hundred and sixty-three when her weight lands on something that is not ice or snow. The softness shifts under her foot and she yelps, yanking back her boot and lurching to find her balance.

A dark bundle of rags lies at her feet, half hidden under a dusting of snow.

"Mary, mother of God," the bundle exhales in a soft rattle. "Have mercy." An arm extends up toward her, and a claw rising out of a blanket grasps feebly at her coat.

Terrified, she bats it away. The claw reaches toward her again, but she swats it away with such force that it falls back to the snow and lies there, still. Marina's heart is thudding dangerously in her chest. She feels herself floating in a weightless panic, with the snow swirling around her face. She cannot think, cannot form any thoughts except that this wraith is trying to take her down. People fall and they die where they have fallen. She must not let it happen. She must not die here in the street. She must get back to the museum.

And then she sees the eyes, two hollow eyes peering up at her from above a paisley headscarf wrapped around the face. The eyes are pleading silently with her.

She knows she cannot lift the woman. She hasn't the strength to get her onto her feet, much less help her to walk.

"I'm sorry," she says. "I can't help you."

The eyes do not shift.

Marina feels again the weight of the chocolate in her pocket. It won't make any difference, she tells herself. The woman is going to die. You can't help her. Be reasonable. There are family at home who need also. It is never enough.

But already she is pulling the candy bar from inside her coat and ripping back the foil. She breaks off a chunk of the chocolate and, crouching forward, holds it out toward the woman. The woman doesn't move, but her dull eyes widen almost imperceptibly. Marina peels the frozen scarf away from the woman's face. The mouth falls open, and Marina places a square of chocolate on the woman's tongue.

One of five rooms devoted to the Flemish, this is known as the Snyders Room. It is a large hall, with a box-beam ceiling painted with Florentine ornamentation. Checkerboard parquet floors, et cetera. Really, the room itself is of no consequence. It is what the room contains—the long wall is lined with enormous market stalls displaying every kind of fish imaginable, geese and game birds strung overhead, and venison and rabbits draped in languid piles. And yet another stall with a profusion of vegetables overflowing their baskets. Heads of cabbage, leeks, garlic, and cauliflowers, mushrooms and parsnips, the variety is dazzling. Walk a few feet farther and here is a long table of fruits: bowls of apples, baskets heaped with plums and pears, stalks of artichokes and watermelons spilling onto the ground. The busy excess makes one faint. One could eat for years in this room and never be hungry.

And across the way is more fruit, these artfully arranged like jewels on velvet. Utrecht's gorgeous, plump grapes are at their peak, his peaches so like the things themselves that their scent perfumes the air. And cherries like a string of bright rubies. One could weep.

The tables on the patio are laden with food. Platters of stuffed mushrooms and roasted vegetables, skewers of grilled lamb. Cheeses and smoked salmon and bowls of fruit nested in a bed of ice. There is an enormous white cake displayed on a separate table, tier upon tier of cake with ornately frosted swirls and leaves and roses, very rococo, like the gilt and plaster walls in the Winter Palace.

At each station, Dmitri asks Marina does she want some green salad? A slice of melon? Smoked salmon and pumpernickel? Long before they reach the end of the line, the plate he is holding for her is heavy with food. He guides her into the white tent and through a maze of tables and seats her next to a tired-looking woman in a bright pink dress.

"I'm getting a plate for myself." He takes Marina's purse and places it on the vacant chair to her left, then disappears into the crowd.

"It was a nice ceremony, don't you think?" the woman in pink asks.

"*Da.*" Marina nods in polite agreement.

"When Naureen said Katie and Cooper were doing their own vows, I thought, Oh boy. But they were so thoughtful and

152

simple, just right. My friend Tina—do you remember her?—
when her daughter got married, they wrote their own vows, but
they rhymed. It was awful—*love, dove, above* kind of stuff.
And they had a juggler come down the aisle. I never did figure
out what that was supposed to mean."

The woman's face is familiar, but Marina can't place it.
There are so many faces to remember, to put names to and order by rooms. Sometimes when she looks, all she sees is a vacant wall. It is frightening, this forgetting, like another little
piece of her life slipping away. If she lets all the paintings disappear, she will be gone with them.

"Mama? Here, why don't you eat a little something." Marina's attention is diverted to the plate in front of her.

"I guess these kids have seen that the old words don't
seem to mean much. Till death do us part. They know
better."

After a moment, the woman picks up Marina's fork and
spears a chunk of melon. "How about some fruit?"

Marina nods and takes the proffered fork and puts the
melon in her mouth.

"Do you want some lamb?"

When Dmitri returns with his plate, the woman in pink is
coaxing Marina through her meal.

"How's this for irony?" she says. "Me trying to get her to
eat?"

"She's just tired. So many people, it tires her out."

"Papa, I know. I know about her condition."

Dmitri looks down into his lap and purses his lips. His chest
lifts and falls.

"Andrei and Naureen and I talked last night."

There is a prolonged silence and Marina's attention fades away.

"I wish you'd told me."

"I didn't want you to worry."

"She's my mother."

Dmitri nods like a chastened child.

"You haven't touched the salad, Mama." Marina hears a voice in her ear. "It's tomatoes and mozzarella. You like tomatoes."

No one mentions food. It is bad manners to refer to one's hunger, worse to provoke the hunger of others with memories of meals eaten in the past. But at night, she dreams of feasts. In dreams, she moves inside a Baroque still life, walking down aisles of tables, some heaped with whole fish and glistening hams, others with rabbit and game. The abundance is heady, and she is drunk with the fragrance of apples. Here is a tableau of fruit and flowers, silver bowls heaped with lemons and grapes, and a pomegranate split open to expose a honeycomb of rubies. Goblets are brimming with red and white wines; they glisten with condensation. Next to them, breads and cheeses are carefully arranged on the heavy white linens. For the Baroque painter and his contemporaries, each of these objects was freighted with religious meaning. The red wine and bread symbolize the Eucharist, Christ's body and blood. The tablecloth is Christ's shroud. The glass decanter is the Virgin Mary, so pure that light shines through it. Oranges are the fruit of the Garden, but lemons are the bitter fruit of sin.

Her eyes fall on a peach, so ripe and round that she can almost feel the weight of it in her palm. She cannot remember what the peach symbolizes, but as she reaches toward it, she is stopped by the booming voice of Director Orbeli. He warns her that these are national treasures. "These are the lifeblood of the people. We must cradle them in our hearts and minds until they are safely returned." She is flooded with shame.

When she turns away, a beautiful goddess in a flowing white gown offers her a slice of cake. She leans over and kisses Marina's cheek.

"Don't cry, Gran," she says. "This is a happy day."

Something far away explodes, a small popping sound like a champagne cork. She is waking up. She hears a stirring in the darkness, a few voices murmuring, and then someone at the far end of the shelter lights a candle. There is whispering; a shell has hit the museum. Her eyes follow the wavering light until it is snuffed out at the top of the steps. The darkness returns.

In the morning, Viktor Alekseevich Krasnov is dead.

There is such a fine line between the living and the dead that his death is detected only when Nadezhda brings him his tea and he does not raise himself from his bed. When Marina awakens, she sees Nadezhda sitting on the pallet with the body of her husband draped over her lap.

"He is gone," she says flatly. She doesn't cry, and there is no expression on her face. The tea cools on the floor beside her.

Marina comes and sits down beside her, and they watch the archaeologist as though he might move, though of course he will not. She is momentarily reminded of Veronese's *Pietà,* a sixteenth-century Italian painting depicting the dead Christ hanging in the arms of Mary. In the flickering light of the single candle, the hollows in his face are sunken in deep shadow, and the skin pulled over his nose and cheekbones is like beeswax. She has always assumed that the Italian painter exaggerated the chiaroscuro to heighten the drama, the contrasts of light and dark, warm tones and cold, were so marked, but here it is.

It is strange what one can get used to. Every day now, people around her die, people she knew. At first this was cause for tears, but it turns out that human beings have a limited capacity for grief. Now, when the residents of Bomb Shelter #3 wake up in the morning, someone among them will have expired quietly in the night.

They are supposed to report the death, but if they do not, Viktor's ration coupons can be shared between them for the remainder of the month. This is what Marina is thinking. Though the thought shames her, it persists: two hundred and fifty more grams of bread a day, one hundred and twenty-five grams apiece for the next eighteen days. Some people who lose loved ones are unlucky—the person dies at the end of the month and his death is of no benefit to anyone.

"He was a good man," she says to Nadezhda.

Nadezhda sighs hollowly. "At least the children are not here to see their father like this," she says.

Marina leaves her and goes to the bakery to get their bread rations. When she returns two hours later, Nadezhda seems not to have moved. Olga Markhaeva is sitting next to her, and Marina guesses that it is due to her that Viktor's body has been moved over to the far side of the pallet. A blanket has been pulled up under his chin and his eyes have been closed.

Olga whispers to Marina, "I didn't want her to sit alone. Did you hear? A shell blew out the skylight in the Spanish Hall last night. Every last pane of glass."

Marina nods. News travels fast. In line at the bakery, several members of the Hermitage staff asked Marina to pass their condolences on to Nadezhda. She remembers the bread in her pocket and her ever-present hunger surges. It would be rude to pull out the bread without offering some to Olga.

"Please stay, Olga Markhaeva, and eat. We have extra

now." She unwraps the three thin slices of damp bread from their paper.

Olga quickly averts her eyes. "No, no," she demurs and pats her stomach as though she is full. "I've eaten. Besides, I must go help with the cleanup. Of course it would be snowing." She shakes her head wearily.

"Of course."

All month, it has been too cold to snow. No one can remember such a winter, not even Anya. Minus thirty. Minus twenty-six. Minus thirty-five. But now, when the windows shatter, it warms up enough to snow.

"These people who believe in a god, why would they worship someone who does this?" Olga complains. "Ah, well, don't get me started. Woe rides on woe and uses woe for a whip. I'll leave you two to your breakfast." She pulls herself to her feet and leaves.

Marina removes her bread from the paper and passes the two remaining slices to Nadezhda, who carefully divides Viktor's ration in exact halves and returns a portion to Marina.

They eat the bread in silence.

Marina is already planning what must be done. They will have to fetch water to prepare the body and then find something to wrap it in. There are no coffins left. Even the museum carpenter, who built hundreds of coffins, was wrapped in a blanket when he died last week. There is no wood left for the dead. For now, the best they can do is to take Viktor down to the cellar room beneath the library that serves as the Hermitage's morgue. Somehow they will have to carry him.

After they have finished their bread, Marina takes a bucket outside to the embankment fronting the Neva. She eases herself down the slippery steps to the river and waits in line to draw water through a hole cut in the ice. Full, the bucket is too heavy for her to lift, and she must pour more than half the water back out in order to carry it. Shifting the weight from one arm to the other, she trudges back across the street, through the museum, and downstairs to the cellar. While Marina was gone, Nadezhda has managed to undress Viktor's body. The sight of his emaciated corpse is too awful, too horribly intimate. Eyes averted, Marina helps her to lift his body onto a bench and then pours the icy water over his limbs while her aunt gently washes.

They dress Viktor in fresh clothes and swaddle him in a sheet. With careful stitches, Nadezhda sews closed the shroud. After they have rested, each of them takes one end of the shroud and they try to carry the body through the shelter, but it quickly becomes apparent that they will have to drag it. Even so, they have to stop every few meters. Though the corpse weighs hardly anything for a grown man, it is an awkward bundle, and they struggle to heave it up the steps leading out of the shelter. The sheet catches and tears on the rough stone, and when the body threatens to slide out, they must stop midway so Marina can bind the unraveling end more tightly.

As they pass through the halls on the ground floor, dragging the corpse of Viktor behind them, Marina marks their passage past bare glass cases, past the missing bronzes and funerary of ancient Urartu. The only evidence of Viktor Alekseevich Krasnov's lifework is shadows imprinted on the felt of the shelves. He never finished his book, she thinks. The pages of the unfinished manuscript are still on the desk, and later she will have to determine what is to be done with them.

Here, entombed in a glass showcase, is Viktor's twin, another desiccated skeleton, leathery skin and bones with a length of linen draped over the hips. The mummy of the Egyptian priest Petese, it was left behind in the evacuation. The living that remained behind have suffered from the ravages of a relentlessly bitter winter, but the mummy, other than exuding a little salt which is regularly wiped off, is just as it was three thousand years ago.

When they enter the mortuary, Marina tries not to notice all the other swaddled corpses lining the room. They place Viktor's body in a corner. Nadezhda slumps down beside the remains of her husband and closes her eyes.

"Come," Marina urges and tugs gently at her aunt's coat. "You must get up." She is afraid that Nadezhda will simply die beside her husband. "We will go out tomorrow," she promises her, "and see about finding a coffin. We will bury him next to his mother and father." She has little hope that they will be successful. Even if they could manage a coffin, there is nothing to pay a grave digger. But she would promise anything now.

Nadezhda opens her eyes, and they travel slowly up the length of Marina's outstretched arm.

"I won't be able to do it alone," Marina threatens.

Nadezhda nods, her eyes vacant and listless, and she holds out her hand for Marina to help her to her feet.

When they reach the staff entrance and step into the cold air, they are breathing heavily. Their breath rises in vaporous puffs. Nadezhda coughs and Marina hears the rattle. They stand for a moment in silence, looking out across Palace Square. It is a Tuesday afternoon, it has stopped snowing, and there are no new tracks in the entire square, no sound except for the rap of hammering on the roof above them. Soldiers have come to board over the shattered skylight.

The sun is setting already, and the clouds are tinted pink on their undersides.

"When I go, you must try to bury me beside him," Nadezhda says.

Marina nods. It would be pointless to argue that neither of them is going to die. Already they move through their days like ghosts, one foot in front of the other, thin as vapor.

No one weeps anymore, or if they do, it is over small things, inconsequential moments that catch them unprepared. What is left that is heartbreaking? Not death: death is ordinary. What is heartbreaking is the sight of a single gull lifting effortlessly from a street lamp. Its wings unfurl like silk scarves against the mauve sky, and Marina hears the rustle of its feathers. What is heartbreaking is that there is still beauty in the world.

Helen is startled out of sleep by the sound of knocking. In the unfamiliar darkness, she gropes for the lamp and snaps on the switch. The travel alarm on the bedside table reads 2:39. The knocking at her door is soft but persistent, and then she hears her father's voice.

"Elena? Elena?"

She wrestles off the cotton coverlet, stumbles around the bed, and then struggles groggily with the chain on the door before she can open it.

Dmitri is standing on the other side of the door, in the dimly lit hallway. An old wool robe is open over his thin pajamas. Tufts of white hair sprout at wild angles from his scalp, giving him the appearance of a lunatic. His translucent, gnarled feet are bare.

"She's gone," he says.

"Gone? What do you mean?"

"I woke up and she wasn't there. I put the suitcase in front of the door, but she moved it."

"Is she in the bathroom, Papa?"

"No." His shaky fingers fiddle with a loose end of the robe's belt. "I went up and down the halls and to the lobby. She's gone." Dmitri's eyes are rheumy, and Helen sees again how very frail and elderly her father is.

"It's okay, Papa. I'm sure she's around somewhere." Her voice exudes calmness, the voice that used to soothe her boys when they had taken a bad spill off their bikes or the monkey bars. "Here, sit down." She grabs some clothes off the chair. "I'll get dressed and go find her."

Her father looks at the chair blankly but doesn't sit. "I was so tired. Usually, I hear her."

Helen takes the clothes she is holding and disappears into the bathroom. She keeps talking through the door as she changes.

"She's done this before?"

"She gets up and wanders the house at night sometimes. But she's safe there. I put covers on the door handles so she can't open them."

Helen splashes some water on her face, runs a comb through her hair, and emerges from the bathroom dressed in the slacks and shirt she wore yesterday. She slips on a pair of sandals.

Dmitri is too agitated to wait in his room, even after Helen explains that Marina might come back and he should be there. So she waits while he puts on pants and shoes, and they leave the door of the room ajar just in case. The two of them check the halls one more time before they descend the stairs into the lobby. Despite her father, Helen has somehow fully expected to find Marina sitting quietly in one of the high-backed chairs. She isn't there, and there is no night manager on duty to ask if an elderly lady has passed through. Helen walks around the front desk and taps on the door marked "Office." It is locked. Another door, not locked, turns out to be a narrow supply closet with mops and a vacuum and stores of toilet paper.

Outside, a sodium lamp washes Front Street with a peachy light. Helen steps out into the cool night and walks down the sidewalk a few yards in one direction and then the other, peering past darkened storefronts into the shadows cast by their awnings.

"Mama?" she calls. The streetlight is buzzing and she hears the monotonous bark of a dog somewhere off in the distance, but otherwise the only sound is the clack of her sandals on the sidewalk. It comes to her then that her mother may actually have wandered off.

"Any idea where she might go?"

Dmitri shakes his head mutely.

She heads to the corner and looks up Spring Street, sees nothing but a few cars angle parked in front of dark shops, and then she jogs the half block back to the inn.

"Let's get the car. She can't have gotten very far, but it might be faster. Wait here."

Helen uses her room key to unlock the front door of the inn and climbs breathlessly up the stairs. All the way up she debates whether to call the police. Is there even a police force to call on this island? She has no idea, but first she'd better make sure her mother's really gone, she decides.

She checks her parents' room one more time, then grabs her handbag and a sweater out of her own room and returns downstairs. Her father is standing just where she left him, a little old man in a pajama top and unzipped trousers, his shoulders drooping under the weight of his misery. She takes his hand and says lightly, "It's going to be all right, Papa."

They go around to the little lot at the side of the inn and get into the rental car. She starts the car and turns off the static rattle of the radio before they crunch over the gravel and roll out onto the deserted street. No one is out at this hour; the town is asleep under a blanket of thick stars. She rolls down the window and quietly calls her mother's name as they creep down the street. They pass a darkened ice cream parlor and a variety of shops selling clothing and souvenirs and antiques. She stops in front of the ferry ramp and peers out across the black bay. The thought that her mother might wander toward the water unsettles her, but she puts aside that possibility.

Past the ferry dock, the tourist shops begin to peter out, interspersed with bed-and-breakfasts, a diner with its chairs turned upside down on the tables, a real estate office, a Coast to Coast, and a gas station, its self-serve pumps showcased under a stark fluorescent glare. As the street begins to climb up a slope, there are homes set back from the road, shingled cottages adorned with hedges and neat gardens, others more modern and perfunctory. She scans the darkened yards, the halos thrown by porch lights, looking for movement. Beside her, Dmitri is pressed forward against the shoulder restraint, his eyes trained out the passenger window at the houses on the right.

Then they are past town, and their headlights are brushing under thick trees, picking out only the occasional road sign or gravel turnout.

"I don't think she would come out this far," Helen says.

"I suppose not," he says, and slumps back into his seat.

"It's okay, Papa. She's probably just somewhere right around the inn. She may even be back in bed by now." She means to comfort her father, but she herself isn't convinced. Given what she's seen in the past two days, it seems like a bad bet that her mother has it in her to remember her room number, much less find her way back to an inn in a strange town. She flashes on news stories about confused seniors wandering away from their homes and even disappearing for good.

She turns around at a wide spot in the road, and they circle back into town. At each corner, she catches her breath until she can see far enough ahead to know that her mother isn't on this block either. She turns the car onto a cross street and they roll slowly toward the other edge of town.

"Why didn't you tell me about this? About Mama?" Helen tries not to sound reproachful.

Dmitri stares out the front window, blinking and working his lips. They pass a bookstore, a small brick post office, a market. She scans the empty sidewalks and then glances back at her father. A tear is dribbling down his cheek.

"I'm sorry, Papa. I'm not criticizing."

"We've always cared for each other." His voice is thick.

"What does Dr. Rich say? Have you at least talked with her about it?"

"They did some tests. But there's not so much to be done."

Helen steels herself. "Is it Alzheimer's?"

Dmitri nods.

He is blinking furiously now and biting down hard on his lower lip.

Helen pulls the car over to the side of the street and turns off the engine. Silence fills the interior of the car. She takes her father's freckled hand in her own and squeezes it gently. The air seems to go out of him; tears gather in the folds beneath his eyes and spill down his cheeks.

"I don't know what to do," he admits. "She's getting worse. She can't wash herself anymore. She only stands under the water

166

and forgets to soap herself. I'm afraid to leave her alone, even for a few minutes. Last week, she put some plums in the dryer when I wasn't looking. Our underwear came out with pink splotches, and I found pits in the bottom of the barrel."

"Have you told Andrei any of this?"

Dmitri shakes his head. "I promised her I wouldn't put her in a home. You know how he is—he is so sure."

"I know, but he just wants to do what's best. Look, we'll worry about that later. But I'm going to give him a call," she says, and roots through her purse for her cell phone. "I think we may need some help here." She finds the phone but can't locate the piece of paper with her brother's numbers on it. She empties the contents of her purse into her lap and picks through receipts and wadded Kleenex and tubes of lipstick.

"Do you know his cell phone number?"

"Two four six," Dmitri intones. "Six three seven"— he pauses—"twenty-four seven. Twenty-four. Twenty-four something."

While she's dialing information, she starts the car up again and they proceed down the street. The operator informs her that cell phone numbers aren't listed, and at the customer's request the home number isn't listed either. She tries to explain that this is an emergency, but the woman is unmoved and suggests calling 911 if this is truly an emergency.

The night sky is fading imperceptibly to gray at the horizon. Helen clicks the phone off and thinks a long moment before she redials information and asks for the local police.

The voice that answers the phone is gravelly with sleep.

"Is this the police?" she asks.

"Island County sheriff, ma'am. Deputy Kremer."

Helen hears his muffled voice telling someone to go back to sleep. She apologizes for disturbing him and then explains that her mother is missing.

"How long has your mother been gone?" he asks.

Helen checks the clock. It is almost four. "A couple of hours, at least. My father woke up and she was gone."

"Are you sure she's missing? Could she have just stepped out for some reason?"

"She's eighty-two and she has nowhere to go in the middle of the night." Helen tamps down the impatience in her voice. "We're visiting here. There was a wedding. My brother, Andrei Buriakov, has a place here."

"Buriakov?" If the name registers with the deputy, he doesn't let on.

"We've been driving all over, and I'm a little concerned something might have happened. She has memory problems. Alzheimer's."

There is a pause, and when he speaks again, his voice has taken on a new tone, even and official. "Where are you calling from, ma'am?"

"I'm in the car." They are past town again, on a road that seems to be heading out in the general direction of Andrei's, though she doesn't recall what looks like a farm up ahead. "Maybe a mile outside of town," she guesses. "I don't know the road."

"And where was your mother last seen?"

He asks a few more questions, taking down all the information: her name, where they are staying, her brother's name, and then a careful description of her mother. He pauses before he asks, "Any chance she could have gotten on the ten o'clock ferry?"

They stayed at Andrei's last evening just long enough to see the bride and groom off on their honeymoon. Katie had stood on the float of the seaplane and thrown her bouquet back at the cluster of young women crowding the dock. Then the pilot helped the couple climb in and they puttered out into the bay and thundered noisily up into the summer sky. After that, the reception shifted into a party, and Helen and her parents made their excuses. At the hotel, her parents had turned in immediately, exhausted by the day's festivities, but Helen was still up reading at ten. She remembers marveling that it was just starting to get dark.

"I think I would have heard her," Helen says. "Besides, I think she's still in a nightgown. Wouldn't someone stop her?"

"Hard to say. How about we'll meet you in front of the Arbutus. Might take us a few minutes to get over there."

When she clicks off the phone, she tells Dmitri that the deputy is meeting them, and then they turn back and take one last pass through town, past the hardware store, past the Bumblebee Diner with its sign reading "Closed, Come Again!" and past the Kingfisher B&B. A few cars have queued up alongside the road for the ferry. The glassy water of the harbor mirrors a dim gray sky, heavy with fog. A seagull cuts low over the water and drops onto a buoy, unsettling another gull in a flurry of shrieking. She watches the birds, dully aware now of her exhaustion and a clammy coldness.

Many of the rooms have no name, only a number. Look around. The glass in the windows was shattered by an explosion, and the windows have been boarded over, so it is very dark. But perhaps you can just make out the walls and the pictureless frames, like empty eye sockets. Over here is a pile of sand with a shovel jammed in the top. What else? Nothing. Just frames. Nothing.

Back up. Go back a room or two until something looks familiar and start again. There are over four hundred rooms, but they are all nearly empty.

Cold seeps through the filmy cotton of her nightdress. She pulls the thin fabric close around her legs and hugs her arms to her chest, trying to warm herself. Someone has stolen her clothing, her quilted jacket and boots and gloves, though she doesn't remember when.

If she falls asleep, she will freeze. This much she knows. But where she is and how she got here are mysteries. Today, yesterday, even an hour ago, are blanks. She is suspended in the present moment and feeling oddly ephemeral, as though she is adrift on an open sea.

Around her are dark shapes, as thin as limbs, skeletal arms and legs swaying, dancing in the blackness. Terror threatens to engulf her, but then the cold pulls her back and disciplines her thoughts.

She is cold. Cold and hungry. This is familiar.

There is also a scent that is familiar, though she can't identify it, something earthy.

It is dark. Night.

And she is cold. She must not fall asleep. If she falls asleep, she will freeze.

On nights when there is no moon, Leningrad disappears.

From her perch on the watchtower, the edge of the Hermitage roof is merely a theory. The dying city beyond gives off no light. Like a photographic negative, what should be solid is seen as an absence, here a dome-shaped shadow cutting into the glittering pavé of stars, over there two black spires spiking the sky. The only other lights are dim as the stars but closer, tiny yellow lights that ring the edge of the imagined city, the campfires of the enemy at the front.

It is the idea of a city, the idea of a world suggested by the gilded frame that surrounds it.

She feels completely alone in the universe, suspended between the star-thick heavens and a black void below. The stars are not a comfort. It is the solitude of shepherds, unbearably lonely.

Nadezhda died a month to the day after Viktor. A romantic might say that she had died of a broken heart, but that was a sentiment for different times. She lost the will to live, a separate thing.

She could have survived, but she wouldn't make any move to save herself. After Viktor's death, she wouldn't even leave the shelter. The other residents of Bomb Shelter #3 had begun to relocate upstairs, leaving behind the gloom and damp that had grown even more oppressive than the shelling up above. Some went back to their homes, others set up cots in the schoolroom, but Nadezhda could not be persuaded to join them. Marina tried to coax her to return to their old apartment, but she couldn't bear the idea of being there without her family.

So what, Marina wonders now, had made her think that her aunt might undertake a more perilous journey alone?

In January, a road was completed over the frozen Lake Ladoga. Called the Road of Life, it was a slender breach in the blockade through which the city began to evacuate nonessential citizens and to siphon in the most critical supplies from "the mainland," free Russia. When the first truck rolled across the lake and entered Leningrad, church bells rang to welcome it.

As soon as the road was operational, Director Orbeli received orders from Moscow to reduce the staff of the Hermitage. One by one, he began calling people into his office. When Marina's turn came, she waited in the hallway outside his closed door.

Even had she not known the purpose of their meeting, she would have been nervous at the thought of standing alone in his presence. She had never before spoken privately with the director beyond meekly returning his greetings when they occasionally crossed paths on their respective rounds through the galleries. With his long white beard and the legends of his unpredictable rages, he was like the Old Testament god, and the prospect of incurring his displeasure made Marina's hands shake uncontrollably.

The door opened and a staff member emerged, her composure collapsing as she crossed the threshold. A voice inside commanded Marina to enter. Sitting behind his desk, Orbeli looked neither stern nor welcoming, only very tired. He gestured for her to sit down in the chair opposite him. Then, in a speech he had clearly repeated many times over already that day, he told Marina that her heroic service to the museum over the winter had not gone unappreciated. The people of the Soviet Union were indebted to her. Now, though, he must ask of her one last service. The museum was to be mothballed, and only a few dozen staff members would be needed to do that work. The rest were to be evacuated out of the city to ease the defense efforts. He would be waiting for letters of resignation on his desk.

"Please don't order me to go." Her voice was so tiny that she wasn't sure he had heard her. He continued to look at her with his hawkish eyes, but his expression didn't change. At last he said, "May I ask why not?"

How could she explain this? Without her here to keep the memory of its art alive on the walls, the museum would be merely another decaying shell. This was not an idea she could voice aloud.

"My work is needed here," she finally stammered.

"I myself will be leaving at the end of the month. Do you consider yourself more necessary to the Hermitage than its director?"

She flushed, and her eyes fell to the floor. She waited, half expecting to be incinerated into a heap of ash on the carpet.

"You are the one whom I've seen prowling the picture gallery?"

"Yes, Iosef Abgarovitch."

"The niece of Viktor Alekseevich."

"Yes."

"He was stubborn, too."

"Yes."

After a long moment, he said, "Well, go on then."

While Marina herself could not imagine leaving the Hermitage, she had seen no reason for Nadezhda to stay, and she formed the plan that her aunt should join the exodus of staff members. Her motives were selfish. She had become weary of the energy it took to endure her aunt's stubborn grief, weary of climbing up the stairs from the abandoned shelter every day. She wanted to move up to the schoolroom where light trickled through an unboarded window. Mostly, she wanted to be free from the ghosts of the dead and her last remaining obligation to the living.

When she broached the subject with Nadezhda, though, her aunt had balked.

"You are not going?"

"Director Orbeli has asked me to stay on," Marina lied. "I am needed here."

"I'm not strong enough to make the journey alone."

"Not alone. Most of the staff will be evacuating as well."

Nadezhda reached for her hand and clasped it with what might have been tenderness but was just as likely fear. "I will stay here with you."

Marina squelched her irritation and patted her aunt's hand. She urged her to consider Tatiana and Mikhail. They might well be somewhere on the mainland, waiting for her. When Marina said their names aloud, however, Nadezhda's eyes remained like two stones.

"Besides," Marina said, changing tactics, "here, you are using up valuable resources. You have a duty." These were much the same words she had heard from Orbeli that morning, but in her voice they sounded not magisterial but arch and impatient.

"I will not be using them so much longer," Nadezhda had replied.

She was true to her word. After their conversation, Nadezhda rapidly deteriorated. When Marina returned to the shelter at the end of her night shifts, she would light a candle, and in the tiny flare of light she would find her aunt just as she had left her, buried under a mound of blankets on her cot. Nadezhda's eyes would blink open and she would answer Marina's greeting. But she made no move to sit up or even to eat. Formerly, the only subject that had held her interest was food, but she no longer spoke of it. She chewed her bread mechanically when it was presented to her, but she didn't savor it. She claimed that she no longer felt any hunger. Her appearance began to change, her face taking on a weird look of concentration, as though she were trying to remember something. Marina recognized the symptoms.

When she was too far gone to object, Nadezhda was finally carried upstairs to the recently opened convalescent center. She was given glucose, but by then it was too late. In the last week, she stopped eating entirely. She had a terrible thirst and in a scratchy voice begged the nurses for something sour to drink. The nurse on duty advised against it, but Marina couldn't bear to watch her aunt's agony. She brought her a cup of vinegar, spooned it down her throat, then watched as she promptly vomited it back up. The next day, she was dead.

Just as she had done when her uncle died, Marina prepared the body and she and Liliia Pavlova dragged it back below-ground to the mortuary. In the interval of four weeks, many more bodies had collected in frozen mounds on the stone floor. She found her uncle's corpse by picking out the sheet she had wrapped him in, and she placed her aunt next to her husband.

The next day, she moved her things upstairs into the school-room. Then she went to the registry office and stood in line to turn in Nadezhda's papers. No one in the long line cried or showed any sign of emotion. They might all have been waiting in a breadline.

Initially, Marina too felt nothing, except perhaps relief, but that quickly passed. She hadn't anticipated how hard it would be to stay on alone. Now, she chastises herself for bringing on her aunt's death. Here in Leningrad, the pull of the dead was too strong, but surely Nadezhda would have evacuated if Marina had agreed to go as well. Instead, Marina had insisted on remaining in the Hermitage and, by doing so, sentenced her own aunt to die there.

For what? Everything that mattered to her has disappeared. For a while after Nadezhda died, she continued to walk the gallery. But hunger slowed her brain, and when she tried to re-cite her memory palace, her thoughts seemed to move through sludge, words falling away, whole sentences lost in the muck. The paintings themselves seemed to be disintegrating, shot through with light and shadow like leaves eaten into lace by in-sects. She would be talking and find that she couldn't actually visualize what she was describing. She might close her eyes and focus her mind, but Caravaggio's *Lute Player* was just the idea of a lute player, not an image.

Now she no longer has the strength to expend on unneces-sary journeys through the museum. The rigors of work, the ur-gencies of the body, and the metric tick from meal to meal absorb what little energy she has left. She must rely entirely on her memory, and, cell by cell, she can feel those memories fading. Even when she is able to reconstruct a picture, it is nothing more than pigment on canvas, without any feeling or meaning. The Benois Madonna, the Madonna with Partridges, they are all just pictures, nothing more, a fable concocted to lull the masses into compliance. That she once prayed to paintings—not even to the paintings themselves, but to the places on the walls where they had hung—seems inconceivably ridiculous. She has stopped asking for miracles; in fact, she can scarcely imagine what there is left to desire.

She is cold. If she falls asleep, she will freeze.

She feels the pull of death. What a relief it would be to relax into nothingness. To follow the long line of souls—Aunt Nadezhda and Uncle Viktor, her parents, her beloved Dima—the throng that has already abandoned the city for other realms. She might simply go to sleep up here on the roof and be gone within the hour.

In the distance, she hears the drone of incoming planes. She no longer feels fear at their approach; the incessant air raids have blunted her fear and taken on the dull quality of other daily routines: standing in lines, eating, sleeping.

When the lead plane, a lighter Heinkel, releases a string of parachute flares, she watches the pink fireflies of light floating, drifting slowly down like a surreal fairy ballet. Shadows of the city leap and dance in their light. A corner of her mind recognizes that what she is seeing is strangely beautiful, but it is an abstract idea, a memory of beauty, and it does not touch her.

She is watching, a dispassionate observer, someone halfway gone already, when she feels something move inside her. She puts her hand on a spot just below her ribs and moves it slowly over her belly. Pressing down on one place, then another, she searches her abdomen as though for an injury. After a minute or two, there is a responding jolt under her palm. She startles and presses back and feels the lump swim away from her hand.

Someone is here with her, not Zeus, but an invisible presence nonetheless, a small life trying to kick its way into this world.

The search expands exponentially all day, mushrooming from a private concern into a full-scale public drama. An incident command post is set up at the high school, and as volunteers arrive in the cafeteria, they are divided into teams and assigned a leader and a swath of the island to search.

The family seems to be cordoned off from the gathering crowd by their misfortune. Though people cast sympathetic sidelong glances in their direction, the barrier is crossed only by officials. Mike Lundgren, the fireman assigned as the family's liaison, comes over to the long cafeteria table where they are sitting, carrying a cardboard tray of coffees balanced on top of a large box of pastries.

"You folks want some coffee and a roll?" he offers.

Dmitri's dull gaze is fixed on some interior distance, and he doesn't answer, but Naureen thanks Mike. She fixes a cup of coffee for Dmitri, prying the paper off a creamer, shaking in a packet of sugar, and setting it in front of him. Then she picks out a muffin for him and a napkin and urges him to have a little something to eat. He stares at the coffee and muffin as though he doesn't register what they are.

Mike looks over a clipboard. "I've just got a few more

questions. Sir?" He waits for Dmitri to acknowledge him. "Just a few more questions. No heart condition, no diabetes or hypoglycemia, right? Medications. What medications does your wife take?"

Helen interrupts him. "We already went over all of this with the sheriff."

"Yes, I'm sorry about this, but I need to make sure it's all accurate for our report. Sir?"

Dmitri looks up, his eyes bleary and slow, and Mike repeats the question twice before Dmitri nods. He recites a list of drugs, unfamiliar to Helen, and then as Mike pauses over his pad, Dmitri repeats them more slowly.

While Mike is writing down the names, another fireman comes over and stands waiting.

"Excuse me just a moment." The two men step a few feet away and confer in quiet voices.

Helen's heart spasms. When Mike returns to his seat, she croaks, "What is it? Did they find her?"

"No, ma'am. He was just telling me they've finished setting up the first teams and they're getting ready to move out."

Dmitri rises and tries to extricate himself from between the bench and table. "I will go with them."

"We've got plenty of volunteers, sir."

"I will go look for her," he repeats.

He looks at Dmitri skeptically. "I'm not sure that's such a good idea. How about we put your son and daughter out there, and you stay here, where we can keep you apprised of the whole search?"

Dmitri isn't mollified. He remains standing, waiting for

Helen to slide out and release him. Instead, she puts an arm around him and coaxes him to sit down again.

"You heard Mike. They're going to find her, and she's going to be fine. But you're not going to help her by wearing yourself out any more," she says.

He is persuaded to stay at the command post only after Helen agrees to stay behind with him, and Andrei and Naureen promise to call periodically and check in.

All morning and into the afternoon, people continue to come and go, filling in log sheets or grabbing a bottle of water before they head back out, cell phones pressed to their ears.

At the edge of the fray, Mike Lundgren has unfolded a couple of canvas chairs for Helen and her father, but Dmitri seems determined to prove that he is fit enough to join the search. Periodically, he gets up and drifts around the cafeteria, offering to help volunteers who are unloading donations: cases of pop and bottled water, boxes of sandwiches and chips and trail mix, even sunscreen and bug spray. He gathers up every rumor or bit of news as it filters in and then reports back to Helen. His latest mission was to check out the arrival of a dozen or so military-looking types, conspicuously outfitted in bright orange caps and vests and shouldering fifty-pound packs, who strode into the courtyard outside the windows about a half hour ago. When he returns, he is escorted by Mike Lundgren.

"They are a professional search and rescue unit," Dmitri tells Helen. "They came on the noon ferry."

"I wonder, do you happen to have your dad's room key?" Mike asks her.

Helen picks up her purse and starts rifling through it.

"The dogs need something with her smell on it," Dmitri

182

says, pointing out a pack of hounds milling excitedly near the door. "They give them something with her smell on it, and the dogs find her."

Helen finds her own key but not her parents'. She can't recall if she ever had it, or if she left their door unlocked. Her brain feels sodden.

"It doesn't matter," Mike says. "We can get one from the desk clerk. Mr. Buriakov, are you sure I can't talk you into going back to your room and getting a little rest? You're looking a little wobbly."

Mike would probably like to get Dmitri out from underfoot, but it's also true that, if possible, Dmitri looks even more disheveled than he did this morning. He's still wearing his pajama top under a windbreaker, and his face is alarmingly ashen.

"I'm okay here," Dmitri says, and sits down to make his point.

"But maybe your daughter would like to freshen up." Mike looks directly at Helen as he speaks, appealing to her as a co-conspirator.

"Actually, that sounds like a good idea, Papa," she says. Dmitri may be past caring, but she is suddenly uncomfortably aware of what she must look like—those victims you see on the evening news who have been rousted from their beds by disaster, a tornado or fire or flood. She runs her tongue self-consciously over her fuzzy teeth.

"I should stay here," Dmitri says, "but Elena, you can go. She can help you choose something of Marina's for the dogs."

Mike, beaten at his game, suppresses a smile. He thinks for a minute. "Well, how about this," he counters. "There's a couch in the school counselor's office. Would you at least lie down there?"

Dmitri agrees, but only after extracting a promise that he will be informed if anything, anything at all, develops. Mike waves down a volunteer.

"Can you find someone to unlock Ginger Cantor's office for Mr. Buriakov? He'd like to lie down for a while."

He turns to Helen and offers his arm as though they are at a dance.

"Ma'am?"

"Please. Helen."

"Helen."

"You know, you don't need to go with me," she protests, foolishly flustered.

"Happy to," he says, and he seems genuinely to mean it.

In the cab of Mike's truck, Helen feels safely out of her father's earshot for the first time today. She asks Mike about the dogs.

"Is it that serious? I mean, they just look so ominous."

Mike nods but doesn't speak right away. "Usually," he begins, "we get a call like this, and the missing person turns up pretty quick, no harm done." He studies the road as though he may find the rest of his words on the pavement. She has noticed that he seems to weigh everything he says, and she wonders if this is his typical demeanor or a caution specially adapted to the situation.

"When it goes on more than an hour or so, you gotta take all the precautions."

"This happens a lot?"

"It happens. We've got a guy takes off every couple of months. He used to be a runner, so he's pretty easy to find. Sticks to the roads mostly."

Mike swings the truck in the fire lane in front of the Arbutus and shuts off the engine. "I wouldn't worry too much just yet," he offers. "Some of them hide like children. Last year, we looked for this one lady for almost eight hours and then we found her under her own house. She was squeezed in a gap behind some shrubbery."

She has heard this story already, from the deputy. Helen does a quick calculation. Marina has been missing longer than eight hours already. She wonders if there are other stories, ones without happy endings.

Upstairs, they retrieve a clean shirt for Dmitri and a pair of Marina's knee-highs, which Mike drops into an evidence bag. He says he'll come back for her later, if she wants to rest or clean up. They're standing in the hallway between the two rooms, and Helen looks at the door to her room.

"I think I'm past sleep," she decides. She's shaky and buzzing on too many cups of coffee, but more to the point, the prospect of being alone with her thoughts is too unsettling. "Can you wait, though, for just a minute or two, just long enough for me to brush my teeth? I don't want to hold things up." She gestures to the evidence bag.

"You do whatever you need to do," he says, and leans back against the wall. His eyes are steady and warm. "I'll be here."

A flush of gratitude nearly undoes her, and she turns away quickly and fumbles with her door key. Inside, she hurriedly brushes her teeth and washes her face. She fluffs up her hair, dabs some concealer under her eyes, and avoids studying her reflection. She chastises herself for her ridiculous vanity. It's not as though he's waiting to take her on a date.

When they get back to the high school, the search and

rescue team has already headed out, and Mike needs to take the evidence bag to them. He points out to Helen where the counselor's office is located, across the courtyard, and promises to check back periodically and keep them briefed.

Dmitri is lying on a couch, but when she peeks into the room, his eyes click open like a china doll's.

"What is it? Did they find her?"

"We were only gone a few minutes, Papa," Helen says. "Were you asleep?"

He shakes his head no and sits up. "Where could she go, Elena?" He has asked this question or some variation of it at least twenty times today.

"I don't know, Papa."

"It's not so big an island."

"Mike says they hide sometimes."

She settles into a deep chair with sprung cushions and flips absently through an old, dog-eared copy of the *Smithsonian* magazine. She tells Dmitri about a glass harmonica invented by Benjamin Franklin. She reads him an article about the great blue heron. He asks her again how come it is taking them so long to find Marina. She repeats the more upbeat theories he has heard already, that she may have found a warm place to curl up and sleep—a toolshed, an unlocked car. There are vacation homes empty all over the island, even in high season. Periodically, Helen gets up and takes another stroll around the courtyard outside.

And so the warm afternoon ticks away into evening. As promised, Mike comes in every hour or so to brief them, even though there's nothing to report. He brings offerings of coffee, sandwiches, bags of potato chips, and fruit and candy, all of which she sets aside but then ends up eating. This is how she marks the slow passage of time, in one-hour increments, each separated into smaller units of Fritos or grapes or Kit-Kat bars. Andrei calls twice to see how they are doing, and Helen tells him that they are doing fine. Later, there is dinner in the cafeteria, trays of lasagna and bowls of three-bean salad and coleslaw provided by the women of Drake Presbyterian.

Eventually, the light drains from the sky outside. At first, it seemed inconceivable that Marina could simply vanish, and though Helen was worried, at some deeper level she believed her worries were unfounded. Any moment, her mother would turn up, confused but unharmed. But with each hour that has elapsed, that outcome has seemed increasingly remote, and now, with the coming of dark, Helen realizes that, on an unconscious level, she is bracing herself against an unspecified horror. Dmitri, too, has retreated back into himself; he no longer asks any questions, and even when Mike comes in he registers no interest. Mike suggests again that they go back to the hotel, but he gets nowhere; Dmitri has set like concrete and will not be moved any farther to the periphery. Instead, a cot and blankets are brought in, though these too seem outside the private conditions of his vigil. If he cannot go and search for his wife, perhaps he can bring her back by force of will.

Helen flips through a magazine, waiting for something to grab her attention. She can't sleep, either, but neither can she focus enough to read anymore. She gets up and crosses over to a rack of pamphlets on the wall: how to prevent sexually transmitted disease, how to recognize depression, how to choose the right college or career, advice against methamphetamine use and smoking and alcohol. She is glad her children are grown. Given the limitless risks, it seems a miracle that any children survive into adulthood—and deeply unjust that one may survive and then find at the other end of life not rest but a new set of dangers.

"Are you sure you don't want the cot, Papa?" she asks. He shakes his head like a slow metronome.

"I think I'm going to try this again." He doesn't respond. She feels guilty, as though she is giving up on her mother or abandoning him.

She walks over to the couch and, sitting down beside him, takes his hand. His mouth shifts a little, but he doesn't raise his eyes or otherwise acknowledge her. His hand is limp in hers.

"We have never spent a night apart," he says eventually.

"What about the war?" she asks.

He brushes the comment off, and she's not about to force the issue. But she doesn't know what else to say, either.

"Well, okay," she says, squeezing his hand, and rising to her feet. "I love you."

He nods. "I love you also, Lenochka."

"Do you mind if I turn off the overhead light? I can leave this lamp on."

Lying on the cot, she stares at the ceiling. A random design of holes is punched into the acoustic tiles. She searches idly for patterns, as one might scan the night sky for crabs and hunters and lions. Here is what might be a face with one eye, there a dog with an enormous tail. Only a desperate need for sense, she thinks, could connect these dots into pictures, or the constellations into a meaningful universe.

In March, the public baths are opened. Marina and Olga Markhaeva wait in line outside the *banya* for three hours, as clusters of women emerge and two dozen more are admitted. In the park across the street, the bulbs that were not dug up and eaten during the winter are pushing spears through the snow. It is still cold, but the bitter grip of winter is loosening. Icicles are melting and crashing to the ground, and each day, the sun stays up in the sky five minutes longer than the day before.

Katya Kostrovitskaia, a worker on the museum's crash rescue team, approaches them as she is leaving. Her cheeks are flushed. "It is marvelous," she tells them. "The steam is not so hot as the old days, and there are no birch branches to make *vaniks,* but feel," she says, and wraps Olga's hands in her own. "They are still warm."

Finally, they reach the front of the line and hand over their tickets. They enter an anteroom with rows of benches where, with a few dozen others, they disrobe. "Deposit your clothing with the laundry workers," an attendant requests. "It will be disinfected and held for you. Your time will be limited to two hours. Please return to the anteroom and collect your clothing before the two hours has elapsed. May your steam be easy."

Marina sits down beside Olga and gingerly begins to remove her boots and roll down the top layer of stockings. She has lived in these same clothes from week to week, sleeping and working swaddled in so many layers that her body has been disguised even to herself. While climbing the Jordan Staircase, she studiously avoids her reflection in the mirrored walls, but when she washes herself in a darkened corner of the shelter, sponging her neck and arms and up under her skirts, she has felt the bones of her body surfacing, one by one. Whether she is sitting or lying, they stab against her skin.

The ring that Dmitri gave her in the fall and which she has never gotten sized now knocks loosely against the knuckle of her ring finger as she rolls down another stocking. She stares with horror at the leg that emerges, its skin like burlap and splotched with blue spots from scurvy. At the end, the foot is as rough and blackened as the pads of a dog's paw. Her stomach lurches, and she shuts her eyes. She rolls down the stockings on the other leg without looking, and then methodically unbuttons and removes first her sweater and then her wool skirt and then the dress beneath it. When finally she peels away the last of her undergarments, she stands naked, feeling the forgotten whisper of air against skin.

She cannot look at herself, but her hands reach for her naked belly of their own accord. While the rest of her has withered, her belly has continued to swell, and her hands have explored the growing expanse with wonder. Now, she waits, her attention focused inward, until she feels a reassuring stirring.

"Mine is distended, too." When Marina turns, Olga is gesturing at her own abdomen. It is as rounded as a piece of fruit. Marina is about to protest, but Olga lowers her voice to a whisper.

"Who would think human beings could look like this and still be alive? Look, you can't even tell the men from the women, except for their penises."

Marina follows Olga's glance down the row of naked bodies opposite them. None of them look either male or female, just an undifferentiated procession of ancient, emaciated carcasses, but sure enough, about halfway down the row she sees a penis resting between two withered legs. The man sits, hands limp at his sides and eyes staring stonily ahead, unashamed. There are too few men left in the city to warrant separate baths, but everyone is past caring, their modesty as shriveled as their bodies. Neither is it modesty that makes Marina avert her eyes to the floor. It is revulsion. These are not bodies but wasted skeletons, rib cages and knobby spines and jutting femurs supported on impossibly spindly legs.

Attendants move down the line of benches, collecting clothing and checking each person for lice, systematically moving their hands over scalps before directing them to a tiled shower room where another attendant explains that the water will run for only three minutes, and they must wash their hair and every part of their bodies in that time. Marina steps under the shower and water streams over her head and batters her skin like a hard rain. She grabs the bar of rough lye soap and scours her feet, then works quickly up her body. She has just enough time to rinse the soap out of her hair before the water trickles to a stop.

Before entering the steam bath, they are handed metal basins filled with water and are cautioned to watch for signs of faintness.

It is like passing into the interior of a cloud and entering heaven. Billowing steam obscures all but the few women sitting closest to the door, but the tiled room echoes with the voices of a hundred. Olga grasps Marina's hand and sighs happily.

Each wall is terraced, floor to ceiling, with benches, and the benches are crowded with the bodies of women, wavering in the steam like mirages. Marina and Olga wade slowly through the fog until they find open space on a lower bench that is wide enough for both of them. Marina sinks down and closes her eyes. She takes in the sensation of heat seeping through her skin and sinking into her bones. Katya was right: it is not like before the war, when the steam scorched one's lungs, but there is nothing more delicious than this feeling, like sliding into a vat of warm honey.

Throughout this winter of record low temperatures, she has felt frozen, the cold a twin torture of hunger. Even huddled under a mountain of blankets at night, her frigid body has shivered spastically against the cold. The only relief is the warden's room, where the stove is always roaring and the staff gathers on any pretext. Director Orbeli himself used to visit there often, talking to the staff members and sipping at a cup of tea. When she comes down from the roof at the end of her shift, she lingers there, listening to the conversations and holding her hands close to the grate until her fingers tingle and burn. That is wonderful, but it pales next to this. Here, her entire body is warm and buoyant, as in a dream. She floats on a current of soft, babbling voices and the hiss of water splashing on hot rocks. She is nearly asleep when a tiny foot or fist jabs her hard in the ribs, and she gasps.

"What is it?" Olga's face looms above Marina, her brow furrowed with concern.

Marina has not shared her secret with anyone, but she decides impulsively to make this present to Olga. "A baby," she says shyly. "I am going to have a baby."

But Olga doesn't congratulate her. Her lips pressed together, she shakes her head slowly.

"You are not pregnant, Marina. It is the dystrophy. You must know that."

"No," Marina protests. "My menses stopped, and . . ."

Olga cuts her off, gently. "Dear girl, half the women in here have stopped bleeding. It doesn't mean what you think." She pats Marina on the shoulder, comforting her. "Someday, you will have lots of children." This, too, seems dubious, as there are so few men left to father children, but clearly Olga thinks she is not quite rational.

"I'm not crazy," Marina says and meets Olga's eyes steadily. "Here." She moves her hands across her belly, like radar, feeling for the baby. When she finds him, she takes Olga's hand and presses it on a spot to the left of her navel. "Just a moment. Wait." The two women wait, listening with their hands. After a moment, Marina feels the baby stir. She raises her eyes to Olga's and sees confirmation in her look of astonishment.

"It is not possible," Olga insists, shaking her head. She removes her hand but continues to hold it just above Marina's belly, as though warming herself at the warden's stove. Her homely features soften. "A baby." This woman who knows so many poems finds herself at a loss for words. "Life . . . well, well," she says.

Marina becomes aware that she is being scrutinized by the floating heads around her. There is whispering and sidelong glances as the news is telegraphed around the bath. And then an old woman emerges from the steam and stops in front of Marina. Perhaps she is not really old—it is impossible to tell a starving person's age—but she looks like a crone, her gray hair pasted in wet rivulets to her scrawny shoulders and shriveled teats. In the watery light, she is as pale as a wax figure.

"May I?" she asks, and holds out two skeletal hands. Marina clutches her belly protectively, and Olga waves her hand at the woman.

"Leave her be."

The woman ignores Olga and waits for Marina to answer.

Marina feels the baby inside her, floating in his own warm bath, safe and secure. "Yes, it's all right," Marina finally volunteers, as much to the baby as to Olga. She slides her hands away and exposes her belly. The old woman reaches out, and Marina feels a light skittering touch on her skin. As though rising to the unfamiliar touch, the baby swims toward the old woman's hand. She nods, her dull eyes glitter, and her lips pull into the insinuation of a smile.

"He is very strong," she says. "A boy."

Olga snorts.

"Yes, a boy," the old woman insists. "I have helped deliver scores of babies, some of them in this very bath. And this one"—she pats Marina's belly with affection—"is a boy. Here," she says, "feel how strong he kicks."

Emboldened by the crone, other women have gathered behind her. One by one, they appear through the steam and passively hold out their hands, as though in the breadlines. Marina nods and then waits patiently as each set of hands touches her belly. They are polite: as soon as they feel the baby move, they move to the side for the next woman. They whisper among themselves. Marina hears a woman remark, "Look at her breasts, how full they are." And another says, "How far along do you suppose she is?" One of them, when the baby kicks, crosses herself and announces to those around her, "It's a miracle." There is general agreement.

The old crone whispers in Marina's ear.

"I have bread for you. It is in my coat pocket. I will get it."

"No, auntie," Marina says. "You mustn't."

"He needs to eat," the old woman says, and before Marina can protest further, she melts away into the steam like a ghost.

On the first day the trams are running again, it seems that every-one in the city has come out for a ride. The clanging bells draw them out of their dark homes and offices and into the spring air, and even if they have nowhere to go, they line up along the routes and cheer the approach of the bright red cars. There is no push-ing or shoving as there was in the old days. People wait patiently and they give up their seats to those who are too weak to stand. Some carry bundles of bright flowers in their arms.

From the service entrance of the Hermitage, Marina watches one of the cars rumble by. As though it is a holiday, passengers on the tram wave to her as they pass. She would love to ride out to the edge of the city, but there is too much work to do here. She waves back, then picks up her empty pail and turns back into the museum.

Unlocked from its shroud of winter ice, the Hermitage is thawing. The walls ooze moisture, the ceilings are seeping, and rivulets run down the walls. Snow melts on the roof, dripping through the skylights and spattering muddy water onto the floors below. The enormous population of the Hermitage has been reduced to a skeletal staff of perhaps fifty, mostly old women, and a third of those are recovering in the Hermitage clinic at any given time. Like shipwrecked survivors in a leaky lifeboat, those who can work bail water ceaselessly, but it is slow work and they are barely able to keep ahead of the filling buckets. All morning, Marina has been ferrying pails of the filthy water out of the Skylight halls, through the long, vacant corridors, and down the stairs leading out to the embankment. In ten-odd trips, she has seen no one she knows, only a handful of cadets from the naval academy, carrying pieces of furniture.

She climbs the Council Staircase. Most of the windows in the museum have been boarded over and it is almost completely dark, but she knows her way without sight. As she passes through the long corridor of the Rembrandt Room, she ticks off the former inhabitants as though taking attendance. Flora and Danae, the Father and his prodigal son, the poet Jeremias de Decker, the old man in red, Baartjen Martens Doomer, Abraham and Isaac, David and Jonathon, the holy family. She doesn't have time to stop, but out of the corner of her eye, she sometimes seems to catch a glimpse of a familiar face peering out of the dimness.

She turns into the Spanish Skylight Hall. Its dark red walls once teemed with religious fervor, Murillo's Jacob dreaming a swirl of dark angels, Zurbaran's martyred Saint Lawrence carrying the gridiron he will be roasted on, and wherever one turned, another saint caught up in some terrible ecstasy, their eyes cast upward to the celestial light streaming through the monumental barrel-vaulted skylight. Now, though, the room seems more like an underground cavern or an abandoned mine. After a shell explosion shattered the skylight, it was tented over with plywood lashed to the frame with wire. In the gloom, the room echoes with the dripping of water, and, looking up, she sees telltale pinpricks and slivers of light. The braver women on the repair crew have repeatedly crawled out onto the skylight and tried to seal the leaks, nailing down loose boards and shellacking canvas over the seams, but wind and water continually find fresh weaknesses.

Her boots slap across the muddy floor toward a thin waterfall that spatters noisily into an overflowing pail. She hefts the heavy pail and replaces it with the empty one in her hand. Hundreds of tons of snow are melting on the roof, and it seems to Marina that she is hauling it out one pail at a time.

Her back is aching and she is short of breath. When she first knew she was pregnant, she would forget for hours at a time and be amazed afresh every time she felt the baby move. But now it is a continual presence, pressing into her bladder and against her diaphragm, waking her in the night. The baby is beginning to settle heavy and low, and the nurse says it could come any day now. Marina is of two minds on this. So long as it is in her womb, she can protect it from the world. But already it is two weeks late, and the lake is thawing.

Descending the stairs, she feels for each step, balancing against the weight of the water in her hand and the weight of the child thrust out in front of her. In the winter, she was careful not to fall because she might not have the strength to get up. Now, though, she is not thinking of herself. Everything now is for this child. She is merely a vehicle for something bigger.

She figures she has time enough for one more trip before lunch, but when she climbs the stairs with her emptied pail, she finds herself veering off her path, drawn toward the light and the sound of voices coming from the Hanging Gardens above the Palace Mews. Just five minutes to rest myself, she promises.

The garden, once dotted with flowering trees and graceful statuary, is now stripped bare, the marble fountain standing alone amid raw squares of earth. A cluster of women are on their knees in the freshly turned soil, chattering among themselves like sparrows as they root shell splinters out of the ground and plant rows of seed. One of them notices her and waves. It is Olga Markhaeva. She pulls herself to her feet and brushes the soil off the front of her coat.

"You shouldn't be lugging water." Since Olga learned of Marina's pregnancy, she has taken charge of Marina's care, advising her to sleep with her feet elevated, somehow procuring handfuls of fresh dandelion greens, even accompanying her to a doctor to help her secure a milk ration. The doctor's office was crowded with dystrophics, and it was only through Olga's doggedness that Marina had gotten five minutes of the harried doctor's time.

"I'm fine," she reassures Olga. "Dr. Sokolov said I may continue to work just as I have been. It's healthy for the baby, he says."

"What does he know, the old rooster. You are not one of the serfs on his old family estate. Here, sit down and take the weight off your feet." Olga takes Marina's arm and leads her to a bench against the wall. Marina sinks down gratefully. She draws the rich, loamy smells of earth into her lungs and turns her face up to the weak, watery light of the new sun. She can barely feel its warmth—she doubts she will ever feel completely warm again—but the light prickles at numb nerve endings.

"Dmitri and I used to bring our lunches out here," she says, running her hand over the marble. It is smooth and warm under her palm. "We sat on this bench."

Olga nods but doesn't say anything. There are too many dead for words of comfort. This is just the way it is.

The bench has been moved. It used to be in the center of the garden, under a particularly beautiful corkscrew willow. They would chew on their sandwiches and listen to the plashing of the fountain; little rainbows hung in its mist. Dmitri talked about Hemingway and Babel. The sun danced in the green leaves. The perfume of wisteria hung in the air.

It doesn't seem possible that this is the same place. Last summer, the statues were removed to rooms below, and then the harsh winter killed off all the trees and shrubs. Dead willows were cut down one by one for firewood, and now the honeysuckle and wisteria have been pulled out and the rose beds dug up to make room for vegetable plots. There is nothing left but this bench, the fountain, and, heaped against the wall next to her, a dozen old lilac bushes, soil still clinging to their rootballs. The gnarled limbs are covered with leaves.

"Look. They are still alive," Marina says. The lilacs, planted ages and ages ago for the Empress Alexandra Fyodorovna, have survived. The heart-shaped leaves seem to glow from within, hundreds of hearts pulsing with a beautiful warm green light. She has never seen such a brilliant green.

"It's a pity, isn't it," Olga says. "They leafed out but they didn't blossom. Besides, we need the room for vegetables. One cannot eat lilacs."

Marina leans forward and plucks a single leaf. It is as translucent as a baby's skin, each delicate vein visible, its tender edges just starting to curl inward. She feels something inside her rip open, and the leaf is swimming in a blurry flood of tears.

"There, there." Olga rubs Marina's back tentatively. "Stop, now. You mustn't weep. It isn't good for the baby, so much grief."

Marina shakes her head mutely. She can't explain it, but what she is feeling is as much gratitude as grief, some primal feeling that contains both. "It's not that," she sobs. "I'm here to see it. This green. This day."

In a way, it was easier in winter. The dark, the cold, the hunger, reduced the world to a repeating sequence of dull, small movements. One moved through the day like a zombie, enduring the unendurable, feeling nothing. Now, Marina finds herself awash in sensation. It is like waking from the dead. Her muscles and bones are stiff, but her soul reels drunkenly, buffeted by unexpected memories and by a tenderness of feeling that surprises her.

"It is the pregnancy," Olga says, visibly relieved to have this explanation. "The mother's moods become tidal." She hands Marina a clean rag and watches while she mops her eyes and blows her nose.

"We'll eat. You'll feel better. It is time for lunch, anyway."

The canteen is filled with workers and the murmuring surge and ebb of dozens of conversations. This is new. In the winter, one heard only the shuffle of feet, the slow scrape of utensils, as each diner focused mutely on his food, but as the weather has warmed, meals have started to become social again, with people turning their attentions outward. Marina and Olga stand in line for bowls of porridge and bread and then, carrying their trays, weave through the tables until they spot Anya and another babushka seated at a large table.

Anya is one of the enigmas of the winter starvation. She

was so frail in the winter that Marina did not expect her to survive, yet here she is. She is bone thin and shriveled as an apple doll, but alive.

"Just look at you," Anya says. "This baby must be fat as a little prince," she says. "Here, sit down next to me, dear." She pats the bench next to her.

The porridge is delicious, green and tangy with beet tops.

While they eat, the women chat about the progress of work in the Hanging Garden. They talk about what is being planted, how many rows of carrots and cabbage, how many rows of leeks and onions, what will be ready for harvest first.

"It's just a big kitchen garden, though," Olga says. "It won't be enough to get us through."

Even on a bright spring day, it is hard to avoid thinking forward to next winter. No one talks anymore of an imminent resolution to the war. The Red Army's victories in December buoyed the population for months, but despite a full-scale offensive, the winter campaign has ended in a stalemate, and the army is near collapse from exhaustion.

Meanwhile, spring is melting the ice road over Lake Ladoga and the only means of escape out of the city. Though the trucks continue to roll along the road, already their wheels are splashing through water.

"If the warm weather holds, they say the road may close within a few weeks," Marina tells Anya. "Dr. Sokolov said I would be able to travel about a week after the birth, but the baby is already two weeks late." Her plan is to travel south to a little resort town in the Caucasus, where many of the Hermitage staff have already headed.

"God will provide, dear," Anya says.

"I don't want to be disrespectful, but after all you have seen, how can you say that?"

The old woman's expression is so full of anguish that Marina is instantly sorry to have challenged her.

"I don't know what He will provide for you, dear. The future is always written with a pitchfork on the water. But I will pray for you. It will do you no harm anyway."

Olga bids them a good afternoon and heads back upstairs to the garden. Marina walks with Anya out to the courtyard. It is strewn with furniture: rows of gilt chairs, Russian Empire settees and divans. The upholstered furniture in the museum has begun to bloom with mildew, and because the staff is too weak to heft the heavy pieces, cadets from the naval academy have been brought in to help move them all into the sun to air. A few old women are working on the upholstery with brushes, dusting a green fur off the brocades and velvets.

Anya claims a comfortable armchair and asks Marina to help her remove her boots. Marina squats at her feet and pulls a shabby felt boot into her lap. The laces are frayed to threads and so knobbed with knots that it is slow work unlacing them. She is careful not to tug hard, lest the boot fall apart in her hands.

"The stockings, too, dear, please," Anya says, leaning her face back into the sunshine and closing her eyes. Marina rolls down the old woman's heavy stocking, exposing a blackened foot. Anya wriggles her toes and sighs luxuriantly.

"It is good to be alive on a day like this." She sinks back into the armchair, propping her bare foot on another chair and lifting her other foot like an expectant child waiting to be undressed by her nurse.

By the time Marina has stripped the second foot and set it

gently next to its neighbor, Anya's chin is drooping on her chest and her eyes are closed. Her face is soft, and saliva burbles on her open lips. It is the privilege of the old, Marina thinks. She tells herself that if she lives so long, perhaps she will be able to sleep like that again.

In the space of an hour, the dozens of buckets and urns in the Spanish Hall have overflowed, creating a sea of mud where they've mixed with the sand.

On her second pass upstairs, she hears the nearly forgotten sound of laughter. She follows the sound through the Skylight halls and into the Knights' Hall, where a pair of boys wearing the blue uniforms of the cadets are peering into a huge show-case, their noses pressed against the glass. Inside are three stuffed horses and the padded forms of knights stripped of their medieval tournament armor and looking like dress dummies.

"You should see them with their armor," Marina says. The boys startle at Marina's voice and back away from the case guiltily.

Smiling, she tries to put them at ease, but their faces remain solemn and unreadable.

"They don't look like much now, but they are quite fierce when they're dressed. Even the horses wore armor." Marina describes the jointed full-body armor, the heavy visored hel-mets, and the breastplates that protected the horses.

The younger of the two boys, only a few years older than her cousins, asks shyly, "Are they real?"

"The horses? Oh, yes, they're stuffed."

The older boy stands rooted to the spot, his glance darting nervously between Marina and the door behind her.

"It's okay," she reassures him. "You're supposed to stop and look. We all do. I'll tell you what: when you're done, would you like me to show you what else we have here?"

The boys hesitate.

"I don't know if our captain will allow it," the older boy volunteers.

"I'll speak to your captain and to mine. It seems like the least we can do to thank you for all your help."

"Yes, auntie," the older one says to her. It is the common-place term used to address any older woman, but Marina has to resist the urge to hug him.

"Good, then. It's settled."

Green. The word doesn't begin to describe this.

For the moment, she forgets that she is lost, that she is weak and chilled and the soles of her feet are tender with sores. She pinches a leaf between her thumb and forefinger and holds it up. It is breathtakingly beautiful, the first new green of the world, the light of creation still shining inside it. She studies it. Time recedes, and she floats beyond it, absorbed totally and completely in this vision. Who knows how much time has passed? She is beyond the tyranny of time. Dmitri once left her sitting in a chair by the window and returned later to find her still entranced by the dance of dust motes caught in a shaft of late-afternoon sun. He claimed to have done three loads of wash in what felt to her like an instant.

This slow erosion of self has its compensations. Having forgotten whatever associations might dull her vision, she can look at a leaf and see it as if for the first time. Though reason suggests otherwise, she has never seen this green before. It is wondrous. Each day, the world is made fresh again, holy, and she takes it in, in all its raw intensity, like a young child. She feels something bloom in her chest—joy or grief, eventually they are inseparable. The world is so acutely beautiful, for all its horrors, that she will be sorry to leave it.

Helen drifts in and out of sleep, losing consciousness and then starting awake moments later as though she were in danger of drowning. When the sky lightens again, she checks the clock. It is almost five. Twenty-six hours now since this thing started, another hour or two on top of that since her mother disappeared into the night. She sits up slowly, testing her stiff limbs and neck. Dmitri is prone on the couch, his face slack with sleep and his chest lifting and falling rhythmically. Like a mother with a fussy newborn, she slides quietly off of her cot and sneaks out of the room.

The cafeteria is nearly empty: only a silver-haired man with the ropy build of a hiker whom she recognizes as the search coordinator, and Mike, who is stretched out on a narrow bench, his eyes closed, remain. It occurs to her that he, too, has been here nearly a full day, and she wonders if anyone is waiting for him at home. Rather than wake him, she asks the coordinator if there is any news. He shakes his head, his face etched with compassion. "I wish I could tell you different. But that's a crackerjack team out there. And the temperature's stayed warm enough at night. I think we've got lots of reason to feel hopeful." He holds her gaze and adds, "I've been told she's a tough lady. I'm looking forward to meeting her."

Helen's heart, already softened to a pulp, swells with gratitude at all the hidden goodwill in the world. "Thank you," she says, her throat closing around the words. They seem insufficient, but he accepts them with a nod.

She wanders dim halls lined with lockers and trophy cases and peers into empty classrooms. At the end of a hallway, she happens on the art room. She finds the light switch, and rows of fluorescent tubes sputter and buzz to life. There is something enormously comforting and familiar in the industrial room, with its linoleum floors and paint-spattered tables, the open metal shelving, and the pottery wheel squatting heavily in a corner. Student art projects are taped to the concrete block walls. She circles the room, surveying the results of various assignments—one in collage, mostly magazine photos and slogans pieced together like so many ransom notes, another in pastels, twenty versions of the same bowl of fruit. They show the typical range of beginners, from the careful, self-conscious drawings of the A students to those whose distended bowls and smeared fruits are almost defiantly raw and unskilled.

She got her only A's in art classes, to the dismay of her parents and those teachers who had taught her older brother and were expecting an echo of brilliance in his younger sibling. Instead, she was ordinary. She did her homework and met her deadlines because to do less was unthinkable in her family, but she set herself apart only in art class, an area where she had no competition from Andrei. Mrs. Hanson, the lantern-jawed young divorcée who taught ceramics and art, encouraged Helen, even giving her private lessons after school when Helen had used up all her electives. It was in a room not very different from this one that she had been most happy as a teenager.

In an unlocked cabinet, Helen finds a sheaf of butcher paper and a box of charcoal. She sits down at one of the tables and lets the charcoal sail wildly across the empty paper, filling several sheets with nothing but furious black slashes and fast loops and squiggles, just for the feel of emotion streaming through her arm. After a while, she slows her hand and, on a fresh sheet, begins dipping with more tentative, exploratory strokes. She closes her eyes, opens them again, and with more confidence lays down a long, sensuous line and then another.

The head of a young woman is emerging on the paper. She is posed in half-profile, her chin lifting slightly and her eyes gazing up wistfully at some point above and to the left of the viewer. Her hair is pulled back neatly, exposing a slender neck that ends in a plain round collar. She is achingly, slowly beautiful, like the notes of a cello.

It is an image as deeply encoded in Helen's memory as certain vaguely disturbing illustrations from childhood picture books. A battered old photograph in a silver frame on her parents' dresser, a studio portrait from the thirties. She was told it was her mother, the only image of her that had survived the war, yet the girl in the photo bore no resemblance to Helen's actual mother. Besides being impossibly young, the girl wore an expression that was not one Helen recognized, the dark eyes soft and as romantic as a poet's. She didn't think her parents were lying, exactly, but neither could she reconcile this sepia-toned girl with the sturdy woman in shapeless housedresses who cooked liver and onions and ironed gift-wrap and ribbons to be reused. Her imagination failed her.

Now, though, looking at what is very much a re-creation of the photograph, Helen recognizes certain unmistakable features, the wide cheekbones and the firm line of the young woman's mouth, features that give her parents' claim an eerie suggestion of truth. She can't see her mother, really, but one could make the case that this is a younger lost relation.

Helen finds a can of fixative in the cupboard and sprays the drawing to keep the charcoal from smearing. Then she pulls out a fresh sheet and begins again, sketching out the shape of a head, the curve of a shoulder. The rough outlines of another head appear, tilted at the same angle as the first.

She is practiced at working from memory. She used to draw her boys incessantly, starting when they were babies. When they got older and began refusing to pose, she continued on the sly, memorizing their features and putting them on paper later. Sometimes they would catch her looking at them too deeply and moan impatiently, "Stop drawing us, Mom."

But she has never drawn her own mother, never looked at her with the intent to draw her, and it is harder than she would have expected. Her mother's face is so familiar that she can't see her. She abandons one sketch and starts another, and then another. Slowly a face emerges that resembles her mother, though she is too young, somewhere in middle age. The planes of her face are too full, the lines too strong. With her pinkie, Helen softens the line of the jaw into shadow and pulls smudges of charcoal down the throat like gullies. She lays down a veil of delicate hatch marks around the eyes and mouth and adds wispy strokes, the hair that lifts like white smoke off her mother's scalp.

The drawing is accomplished, but in some ineffable way it

misses capturing her mother. Helen studies it, vaguely dissatisfied.

There are voices outside. A search team is coming back in, a dozen or so people trudging across the courtyard toward the cafeteria. She can't make out what they are saying, but their bodies speak poignantly of weariness. As she watches, a church van pulls into the circular drive and unloads another group.

She drops the charcoal and, leaving the drawings behind, jogs up the hall toward the counselor's office, her heart pounding. She shouldn't have wandered off; she should be there with her father. The door is open, but he is gone.

People are streaming into the cafeteria, unloading backpacks, guzzling water, sitting on the floor and pulling off shoes.

She asks the first person she sees what is happening.

"They found her. She's alive."

She hasn't cried, not since this thing started, but now she is fighting back tears, wiping them away as they spring to her eyes. "I thought . . ." Something breaks loose inside her with a guttural sound, and then she is sobbing out grief she has stored for years, her chest racking and heaving.

There are perhaps three dozen boys and a handful of their elders, gaunt old men in faded uniforms. Marina has gathered them on the landing of the Jordan Staircase, just as she used to before the war, though this time she has brought with her two kerosene lamps.

"Welcome to the State Museum of Leningrad, familiarly known as the Hermitage," she says. "Over a million visitors pass up these stairs each year. The staircase was designed by the architect Francesco Bartolomeo Rastrelli in the eighteenth century. Note the lavish use of gilded stucco moldings, the abundance of . . ." She falters and her eyes drop to the floor. Flakes of paint from the ceiling litter the steps.

The staircase, once a light-filled confection, is gloomy. In March, a bomb blast shattered all the windows, and they are covered over with plywood. The mirrors are clouded with moisture, and the gilt on the railings has dulled and begun to peel away, exposing rusty metal underneath. Marina notes that the painted Olympian clouds above are nearly black.

When she starts speaking again, her voice is softer and less confident. "So much has changed with the war." Her eyes travel from face to face. They wait expectantly.

"I can show you what is still here, but you will have to use your imagination to see the rooms as they were before. This staircase"—she pats the marble balustrade—"was so magnificent. It was like a fairy-tale staircase. Do you remember when Zolushka dropped her glass slipper as she left the ball? Doesn't this look like the staircase where she would have dropped it? And on the ceiling . . ." She gestures upward. "Well, it is very dark, but if you look up, perhaps you can make out some of the Greek gods and goddesses looking down on us." The boys peer up into the blackness above and, squinting, try to detect the figures.

"Can you see them?" She points. "Over there is Zeus with his thunderbolts. No?"

On the spot, she devises a new tour for the boys and their teachers, starting with what remains in the denuded museum.

"Follow me," she says, "and stay close to me or the captain. It's treacherous in the dark if you don't know your way."

She leads them down the Rastrelli Gallery, once a confection of receding arches and light, now a dark maze stacked high with crates, the art bound for the third train that never made it out of the city at the start of the war. They turn left through the Hall of Egyptian Art, passing between a pair of imposing black granite sarcophagi, and from there they descend narrow service stairs into a cellar.

"Watch your step," she says. "This is the repository of Western European statuary," she announces. She holds up her lantern to reveal a low-ceilinged room crowded with marble angels and nymphs, Roman senators and queens. "They were brought down here to keep them safe from the bombs." The statues are arranged in rows facing the same direction, full torsos on pedestals in the rear, busts down in front. A pensive young woman, a hand to her cheek, is seated next to a gallantly posed war hero; the bust of a handsome Roman gazes over the head of a young maiden. A prone Satyr lounges in the front row. In the hissing light of the kerosene lantern, they look like an audience at the cinema watching a silent film.

The boys take turns stepping into the small room and looking at the statues.

"Who's that in the second row?" she quizzes them.

"Catherine the Great," they respond in a chorus.

"And there is Aphrodite. And Cupid."

They cross under the Hanging Gardens and into the New Hermitage building, where she gathers them in a half circle under the rim of a gargantuan vase that dominates the center of the room. The lip of the vase looms high above their heads.

"This is called the Kolyvan vase. It is made of green jasper and is generally considered to be the finest example of Russian stone carving. The craftsmen of the Kolyvan Lapidary Works created this especially for a room upstairs, but it is made of nineteen tons of green jasper, and it was feared to be too heavy for the upstairs. 'Maybe we should just leave it here,' they decided. All spring, it has been filling up with water from the leaks, and every few days the staff here must climb a ladder and bail it out. But we are thinking of turning it into an enormous birdbath," she jokes.

The boys look at her, solemn-eyed, and nod as though this is a reasonable solution.

They are very serious, even the younger ones. At first Marina wonders if they are bored, but they don't fidget or whisper or surreptitiously punch one another's shoulders as boys will do.

When Marina talks to them, they listen raptly, taking it all in with their deep, round eyes. In their young lives, they have already seen too much, and it has given them a slow and haunted demeanor. Even so, they have never seen things such as this. Their eyes widen at each new wonder.

They trail after her through the dim Jupiter Hall, crowded with hundreds of vases made of precious metals and stone and presided over by the towering gold and marble statue of Jupiter. It is like being undersea, with muted light filtering down through a few unbroken panes just below the ceiling and reflecting off the green stone walls.

"The walls are artificial marble," she informs them, "made by a special process mixing marble dust and concrete and dyes. Each of the rooms down here has walls of a different color: here rose colored"—she gestures as they pass through the Ancient Courtyard—"and up here, in the Hall of Dionysus, it is the color of coral. This is a wonderful room. I think it is like being inside the mother's womb, very red and dark and safe.

"Do you wish to see more?" The boys nod, mute but eager.

The captain, an elderly man in a long fur-collared coat, speaks up. "You are very generous, comrade, but we don't wish to overtire you in your condition."

She assures them that she is not tired at all, and, amazingly, she is telling the truth. She feels as though she could walk her charges through every single room of the museum if only they would follow. There is so much she wants to show them. So she leads them up the Main Staircase to the picture gallery on the first floor, holding up her lantern to guide them. Their footsteps echo on the parquet floors. Rows of dusty gilt frames line the barren walls.

"This is my favorite part of the museum, though it may be hard to see why. From here on out, you will have to rely entirely on your imagination."

She walks them into the Rubens Room and stops before an empty frame. The boys look bewildered. Drawing a deep breath, she silently wills up the image. Gradually, a picture takes shape for her inside the frame. It is Rubens's portrayal of Andromeda being rescued by the warrior Perseus. A wonderful winged horse slowly surfaces on the blank green wall inside the frame. Then the decapitated head of the gorgon and the open mouth of the sea monster in the foreground. This will appeal to boys, she decides.

She begins to sketch out the painting for them. Starting at the left edge, she describes the beautiful princess posed with one hand shyly covering her privates, her eyes downcast before the smitten Perseus.

"She is a princess and was about to be sacrificed to a sea monster. Perseus just happened to be flying over the sea on his winged horse—he had been off killing the evil gorgon, whose head is impaled on his shield here. The head is still alive and the face is terrified." She makes a horrible face. "So Perseus looked down, and he saw the beautiful Andromeda chained to a rock, and he fell instantly in love. He flew down and rescued her by slaying the sea monster. Here, at the bottom of the painting, is the dead monster. He is green and very ugly, and his eyes are bulging."

As she talks, she sees that one of the boys in particular is transfixed, a flush spreading across his cheeks. She is encouraged. She asks them to picture the angel placing a wreath on the hero's head and the little putti that busily attend the scene.

They are draping garments over the modest young woman and holding the reins of Pegasus, the winged horse.

"This one little putto looks frightened that he will be stepped on. Pegasus is such a lively horse. His flesh is slick and quivering, and his hooves are lifting off the ground. He has huge white wings, and they are poised for flight. Any second now he will lift into the sky. You can just feel it. In fact, everything in the painting is moving. You almost feel that if you turned away, and then turned back again, the painting would be different." She moves on, but as she walks away she sees that one of the younger boys has lingered behind. He whips his head back and forth as though he may catch a glimpse of something if only he is fast enough.

She skips down a few frames and holds up her lantern. "This is the spot where the painting *Bacchus* hung. Does anyone know who he was?"

One boy volunteers that he was the Roman god of wine.

"Yes, that's right. So this is a picture about drinking. Bacchus is holding up an enormous gold goblet, and it is being filled by one of his Bacchae. The Bacchae were his female attendants. And poised directly under the goblet here is a young cupid catching the spilled wine in his mouth, and another one here is urinating." She sees one boy stifle a smirk. "Over here is Pan, and he is pouring a river of wine into his open mouth. They are all very drunk. Look, even the leopard is drunk." She corrects herself. "In the painting, there is a leopard right here under Bacchus's foot, and he is chewing on a grapevine like a drunken kitten.

"Now, usually Bacchus was portrayed as a slim and handsome young man, but Rubens shows him here as very fat. Imagine a very fat, naked man with flesh piled in rolls on his huge belly. This was painted at the end of Rubens's life, when he was so sick with gout that he could hardly grasp a brush."

The boys trade glances between themselves.

"Excuse me, comrade—what is gout?"

Of course these boys have never heard of such a thing. "It is the disease of the decadent bourgeoisie, caused by indulging in too much rich food and wine. Catherine the Great also had gout. It caused the extremities to swell painfully. Here Rubens has given Bacchus gout, as well. He is seated on a wine cask because his toes are too swollen for him to stand."

One of the boys raises his hand and asks, "Is his female comrade naked also?"

"Well, no," Marina answers, keeping her face straight, "she has only one breast exposed, but that is an astute question, because Rubens's women are often unclothed. He was the undisputed master at painting skin and making it look real, and so he was famous for his nudes."

"Are they pretty?" another boy asks.

"I think they are quite beautiful."

As she moves down the wall, she points out Venus and Cybele, and the boys focus intensely, as though willing the naked women to appear.

In the next room, she stops in front of another vacant frame.

"Oh, I like this one very much. It is called *Saint Luke Drawing the Virgin*. There were so many paintings of the Madonna in the museum, but this one is particularly clever because it is not so much about the Madonna as it is about the artist and art itself.

218

"The people who commissioned van der Weyden wanted an official painting for their guild, which was like a union. They said, 'Paint us a picture with the Madonna.' So over on the left here, holding her child, is Mary." Marina describes a woman wearing a dark, rather plain gown, very similar in color to the dark background.

"But the artist didn't want to paint just another Madonna, because this was such a commonplace subject, so he cleverly put himself into the picture, disguised as Saint Luke, the patron saint of artists. A patron saint," she adds, "is the dead person that believers prayed to for help." With the flat of her hand, she sketches the space on the right that the figure occupied. "He is over here, holding a small canvas and a brush. But not only has van der Weyden put himself in the picture, but he's dressed in bright red, from his head to his toes. So our eye is drawn to him rather than to Mary.

"And then our eye moves here, to the center of the painting. Do you see these two smaller figures in the background?" She catches herself, realizing that she is pointing to a blank square, but the boys and their teachers are all completely focused on the spot where she has directed their gaze. "There are two figures, a man and a woman. They are standing outside, past the studio where the artist is painting his model, and they're gazing away from the viewer at the landscape beyond. They're posed between two dark pillars that open onto a light-filled landscape. Our eyes follow theirs to the view of the peaceful river. It zigzags through a beautiful medieval city and off into this very soft, luminous horizon."

She is awed by the vision and doesn't say anything for a moment. They all stare at the wall in silence.

"So," she resumes, "the artist was saying to us that this isn't really about a Madonna. The real miracle is the painting itself, which lifts us and carries us away to this magical world."

And then she is walking again, backtracking through the rooms. "I have something else wonderful to show you," she promises. She marches them briskly through the empty Snyders Room, calling up in her memory and then reluctantly rejecting canvas after canvas. They are wonderful—enormous market scenes teeming with dizzying heaps of fish and baskets of produce—but it would be cruel to describe such pictures to starving boys. Similarly, she skips past the frames that held Fyt's still lifes, with their artful arrangements of dead game and glistening fruit.

They pass into a dark passage lit only by Marina's kerosene lamp. At the start of the war, the Raphael Loggias, a glassed arcade with exquisitely detailed frescoes covering every surface, were boarded over from the inside and sandbagged up to the top of the windows. The frescoes were left in place, though, and as they move down the darkened tunnel, fantastic images emerge from the shadows, wavering in the dim light and then receding again. Painted squirrels climb columns decorated with elaborate scrolls of oak leaves. Greek athletes strike poses in medallions on the walls.

"This loggia is five hundred years old. It is an exact copy of the original in the Vatican, which was painted by Raphael and his students. This style of ornamentation was seen in classical Rome and was called grotesques."

Every surface is crowded with animals and fruits, with real and imaginary creatures—a porcupine, a crow, a unicorn and a satyr, lions' heads and equestrian mounts and winged angels—an illustrated encyclopedia of the world. The lamplight flickers in water-darkened mirrors, and as they pass, their own images jump out at them. Above, in a succession of vaults, loom sea-dark scenes from the Bible.

At the end of the loggia, they emerge into another denuded room. She draws them into a half circle around the first in a row of freestanding panels.

"This is the spot that held one of the most prized paintings in the entire Hermitage collection. The painting is called *The Holy Family,* and it was painted by Raphael."

Marina gazes at the panel. "I don't know that I will be able to do it justice," she admits. "It's such a wondrous painting because Raphael took these mythical characters, the Virgin Mary and Joseph and the Christ Child, and he reimagined them as real people, an actual family. If they were real, they wouldn't be gilt and perfect. And so what he came up with was this rather melancholy little family portrait. On one side," she says, pointing, "we have Mary. She is beautiful but very distant and unaware. And quite apart from her, over here, is Joseph. He's much older than Mary. He leans on his walking stick and looks almost frail. Between them"—Marina points to the exact center of the blank square—"standing on his mother's lap, is the Christ Child. He's a mama's boy. He is eyeing Joseph fearfully and his arms are reaching out for his mother. Joseph's expression, I think, is one of resigned disappointment, a father whose child rejects him for the mother."

The boys are staring at the blank square, their eyes unfocused and dreamy.

"They have halos," an older boy murmurs.

"Why yes, they do," Marina responds, a little taken aback. "You have been here before?" she asks him.

The boy's eyes drop to the floor. "No, comrade," he murmurs. "It is just . . ." he points to the framed space, unable to complete his sentence.

Marina is puzzled, but she continues. "One wouldn't notice the halos at first, but they are there, fine as piano wires. It's almost as though Raphael was saying that what sets them apart from any other family is almost invisible. They might be us.

"Now, over here was Raphael's Conestabile Madonna." She leads them to another panel, this one very ornate and gilded like the proscenium arch of an old theater. There is nothing in the center where the stage would be except a darkened square of paint.

"The Conestabile Madonna was one of only three paintings that were packed with their frames. Which is too bad for us, because the frame itself was quite beautiful and elaborate." She describes the frame and then works her way in to the round canvas at the center. "Everything in the painting has been arranged to fit inside the circle," she says. "The Madonna's head is slightly inclined"—Marina demonstrates by tucking her chin just so—"and the shore of the lake and the distant mountains curve into the center."

She sees something that has escaped her notice before. It is very faint, but there seems to be another face hovering in the sky just to the left of the Virgin.

She describes the Madonna before her, how small she is, how delicately colored, her formal, upright posture, the way her heavily lidded eyes are distant and peaceful. And the way that the child appears to be reading the open prayer book in Mary's hand.

"Of course, the logical explanation is that he is simply

attracted to the book, as toddlers are. But Raphael's contemporaries would have seen it differently. They would have seen a miracle."

Just inside the left edge of the frame is the faint outline of another child, a child that is not in the Conestabile. It is like having double vision, as though her memory were blurring. Marina remembers her teachers in school describing a phenomenon called pentimento. Indigent painters would sometimes reuse canvases, covering over inferior paintings with a coat of pigment and then painting a fresh picture. With time, as the oils aged, the old image might appear ghostlike behind the new. An eye would peer out from the folds of a woman's skirt, a piece of fruit would hover in a cloudless blue sky. She wonders if it is possible that Raphael used this canvas before he painted the Conestabile.

A second Madonna is coming into focus, and then there are three toddlers ghosting and overlapping one another, and one of them holds up two sticks lashed together in the shape of a cross. With a shock, Marina knows all at once what she is seeing. It is Raphael's Alba Madonna, the one that disappeared, just as Anya described it. She reaches out to touch the canvas, but there is nothing there, just the paneling.

She turns to the boys, her face radiant. "Do you see?" she asks them. Past them, she can see other paintings in the Skylight halls. Her vision is filling with color and images.

She sweeps through a doorway, beckoning breathlessly for them to follow. The hall is so cavernous that lamplight doesn't reach the far end. Above, the barrel-vaulted ceiling recedes into black. From the darkness comes the steady drip of water hitting water, each drop echoing in the chasm. Except for the enormous frames that line the walls, the vast room is empty.

"Look here." She details for them a dramatic scene, three women surprised at an open tomb by an angel. Then she describes another picture, this one showing the Virgin being taken up into heaven. Then another, the conversion of Saul. As she talks, images appear inside the gigantic frames. The pictures are wild with stormy skies and electric emotion, and as Marina's sweeping gestures paint the scenes, the lantern sways, throwing wild swoops of light up the walls. Figures appear out of the shadows, their robes swirling, their hands raised in amazement.

"All this is yours, comrades," Marina tells them. "Can you see?" She is ecstatic. Her voice trembles when she speaks, but her eyes are bright and calm. "It's all yours."

Ravishing splashes of color pour out of the darkness and resolve into images—paintings that hung elsewhere in the museum, paintings Marina remembers and others that she has only heard tell of. The room is filling with women, with children, with saints and goddesses, and the boys are whispering among themselves. They point at the frames on the wall, at the paintings crowding the edges of the lamplight. The captain is weeping. He is staring at the wall, wiping at his eyes. "Look," he says to no one in particular. "Have you ever seen anything so beautiful?" He points to a spot at eye level on the wall. It is Giampetrino's Madonna, and she is staring right back at them.

Several years hence, when Marina's body is finally winding down, Helen will feel no grief, only a quiet detachment, as though she is waiting for a bus—it is late and she is tired, but she has nowhere she needs to be and it will get here when it gets here. She and Andrei and Naureen and the grandchildren have long since said their good-byes, and Marina herself has left, though no one is able to pinpoint exactly when that happened, only that at some point she was no longer there. It is all over but the waiting.

While she waits, sitting at her mother's bedside and listening to the hoarse rasp of her breathing, Helen finishes another sketch of her, something she does periodically to pass the time. Once she had thought that she might discover some key to her mother if only she could get her likeness right, but she has since learned that the mysteries of another person only deepen, the longer one looks.

The last time she sketched her, her mother was still speaking occasionally. She had asked to see what Helen was drawing, and when Helen turned the pad, she had looked at her portrait without recognition. This was no measure of Helen's artistic skill. By then, Marina didn't know who Helen was, either. She called her Nadezhda. Andrei, too, had lost his identity as her son and become someone else, an imagined suitor with whom she would flirt shamelessly. Only old photographs of herself or Dmitri sparked any recognition. Helen had gone to the dresser and picked up the cracked photograph of Marina taken back in Russia and showed it to her.

Marina studied it long and hard, her face a mask of concentration. "She looks familiar," she said to Helen. "Do you know her?"

"Not really," Helen answered. "Maybe you could tell me about her."

"I think she was one of the Madonnas," Marina said. "But I can't say for certain. There were so many."

It is tempting to see meaning where there may be none. Very often, Marina's blank-faced comments have seemed to carry the weighty truth of Zen koans, and the family repeats them, teasing out the possible meanings and then dismissing their own credulity. There is always, though, the yearning to believe.

There was the morning up on Drake Island when the ponytailed roofer found Marina curled up in the fireplace of a mansion under construction out on Channel Bluff. It was Monday morning, and she had been missing almost thirty hours.

As the young man described it later, he thought at first that Marina was dead. She looked just like a ghost in a horror movie, he said, all gray-faced and wearing a dirty cotton gown. But when he prodded her shoulder, her eyes opened and she started mumbling. He thought she might have had a stroke, but then he figured out that she was speaking a foreign language.

He said something in Spanish—kind of dumb, he admitted, but he had panicked and it was the only foreign language he knew—then he mimed for her to stay where she was and ran back to his truck to call for help. He'd heard about the old lady who'd gotten lost over the weekend, and he figured this must be her. It wasn't every day you ran across an old lady in a night-gown, he explained. So he called the sheriff and he got a flannel shirt out of the back of the cab, and a thermos of herb tea. He got her arms threaded into the shirt and helped her sip some tea, and she looked a little better, kind of dazed but smiling. She started looking around and pointing, first in one direction, then another, and saying something. He looked, but there wasn't anything to see, just two-by-fours and joists, the skeleton frame of the house, and the trees beyond. The young man shrugged, saying *No comprende,* but she was insistent, repeat-ing a couple of words over and over. She pulled herself to her feet and, hanging on to his arm, started kind of leading him around the perimeter of the room, stopping every couple of feet and pointing. He remembered he was worried because she was barefoot and there were nails and wood scraps all over the floor. "Look out," he said, and she nodded, her eyes lit bright, and said, "Look."

"Look?" he repeated.

"Look," she answered, and pointed. "It is beautiful, yes?"

"What was beautiful?" Helen had asked the young man, puzzled.

"Everything, man. That's what was so amazing. There's a killer view of the straits, but she was pointing at everything, you know, this dead madrona tree out back, and these bands of

227

sunlight coming through the roof in the garage." Here, the young man's expression had turned very earnest. "It was like she was saying everything was beautiful."

The doctor said Marina was in shock, but Helen has always preferred the young man's explanation. "You had to be there," he insisted. "She was showing me the world."

ACKNOWLEDGMENTS

Many people have had a hand in shepherding this book along. My grandparents' lifelong love affair and their journey with Alzheimer's provided an initial inspiration. Gratitude goes also to Clifford Paul Fetters, my first and best reader, whose faith never wavered, and to my parents, Beverly Taylor and Ed Dean, for their love and financial support. Thanks to Stuart Gibson and the guides and researchers at the State Hermitage Museum who so graciously answered my endless questions; to Eric Kinzel and Yekaterina Roslova-Kinzel for advice on things Russian; to Cynthia White, Susan Rich, and Linda Wendling for their generous reads; to Mark Elliot for information on the Soviet repatriation; to San Juan County Sheriff Bill Cumming and Undersheriff John Zerby for advice on search and rescue. The Barbara Deming Memorial Fund came through with a grant and the attendant vote of confidence just when it was needed. I am deeply indebted to Claire Wachtel and the good people at William Morrow for their enthusiasm, and most especially to agents Marly Rusoff and Michael Radulescu for voting with their hearts. Finally, to the people of St. Petersburg, Russia, it's my humble intent that this book will honor their great story.

AUTHOR'S NOTE

While the characters in this novel are fictional, the wartime events are drawn from historical records. Readers interested to learn more about the Siege of Leningrad might wish to read Harrison E. Salisbury's *The 900 Days: The Siege of Leningrad;* S. P. Varshavskii's *The Ordeal of the Hermitage*; and Cynthia Simmons and Nina Perlina's *Writing the Siege of Leningrad: Women's Diaries, Memoirs, and Documentary Prose*. The State Hermitage Museum also has an expansive website (www.hermitagemuseum.org) that provides history, digital reproductions of the collection, and panoramic views of various rooms in the museum.